The Bold Dare All

SELECTED FICTION WORKS BY L. RON HUBBARD

FANTASY
The Case of the Friendly Corpse
Death's Deputy
Fear
The Ghoul
The Indigestible Triton
Slaves of Sleep & The Masters of Sleep
Typewriter in the Sky
The Ultimate Adventure

SCIENCE FICTION
Battlefield Earth
The Conquest of Space
The End Is Not Yet
Final Blackout
The Kilkenny Cats
The Kingslayer
The Mission Earth Dekalogy*
Ole Doc Methuselah
To the Stars

ADVENTURE
The Hell Job series

WESTERN
Buckskin Brigades
Empty Saddles
Guns of Mark Jardine
Hot Lead Payoff

A full list of L. Ron Hubbard's
novellas and short stories is provided at the back.

*Dekalogy—a group of ten volumes

L. RON HUBBARD

The Bold Dare All

GALAXY PRESS

Published by
Galaxy Press, LLC
7051 Hollywood Boulevard, Suite 200
Hollywood, CA 90028

© 2014 L. Ron Hubbard Library. All Rights Reserved.

Any unauthorized copying, translation, duplication, importation or distribution, in whole or in part, by any means, including electronic copying, storage or transmission, is a violation of applicable laws.

Mission Earth is a trademark owned by L. Ron Hubbard Library and is used with permission. *Battlefield Earth* is a trademark owned by Author Services, Inc. and is used with permission.

Story Preview cover art: © 1936 Metropolitan Magazines, Inc. Reprinted with permission of Hachette Filipacchi Media. Horsemen illustration from *Western Story Magazine* is © and ™ Condé Nast Publications and is used with their permission. Fantasy, Far-Flung Adventure and Science Fiction illustrations: *Unknown* and *Astounding Science Fiction* copyright © by Street & Smith Publications, Inc. Reprinted with permission of Penny Publications, LLC.

Printed in the United States of America.

ISBN-10 1-59212-306-6
ISBN-13 978-1-59212-306-3

Library of Congress Control Number: 2007903620

Contents

FOREWORD	vii
THE BOLD DARE ALL	1
STORY PREVIEW: FIFTY-FIFTY O'BRIEN	89
GLOSSARY	97
L. RON HUBBARD IN THE GOLDEN AGE OF PULP FICTION	105
THE STORIES FROM THE GOLDEN AGE	117

FOREWORD

Stories from Pulp Fiction's Golden Age

AND it *was* a golden age.

The 1930s and 1940s were a vibrant, seminal time for a gigantic audience of eager readers, probably the largest per capita audience of readers in American history. The magazine racks were chock-full of publications with ragged trims, garish cover art, cheap brown pulp paper, low cover prices—and the most excitement you could hold in your hands.

"Pulp" magazines, named for their rough-cut, pulpwood paper, were a vehicle for more amazing tales than Scheherazade could have told in a million and one nights. Set apart from higher-class "slick" magazines, printed on fancy glossy paper with quality artwork and superior production values, the pulps were for the "rest of us," adventure story after adventure story for people who liked to *read*. Pulp fiction authors were no-holds-barred entertainers—real storytellers. They were more interested in a thrilling plot twist, a horrific villain or a white-knuckle adventure than they were in lavish prose or convoluted metaphors.

The sheer volume of tales released during this wondrous golden age remains unmatched in any other period of literary history—hundreds of thousands of published stories in over nine hundred different magazines. Some titles lasted only an

• FOREWORD •

issue or two; many magazines succumbed to paper shortages during World War II, while others endured for decades yet. Pulp fiction remains as a treasure trove of stories you can read, stories you can love, stories you can remember. The stories were driven by plot and character, with grand heroes, terrible villains, beautiful damsels (often in distress), diabolical plots, amazing places, breathless romances. The readers wanted to be taken beyond the mundane, to live adventures far removed from their ordinary lives—and the pulps rarely failed to deliver.

In that regard, pulp fiction stands in the tradition of all memorable literature. For as history has shown, good stories are much more than fancy prose. William Shakespeare, Charles Dickens, Jules Verne, Alexandre Dumas—many of the greatest literary figures wrote their fiction for the readers, not simply literary colleagues and academic admirers. And writers for pulp magazines were no exception. These publications reached an audience that dwarfed the circulations of today's short story magazines. Issues of the pulps were scooped up and read by over thirty million avid readers each month.

Because pulp fiction writers were often paid no more than a cent a word, they had to become prolific or starve. They also had to write aggressively. As Richard Kyle, publisher and editor of *Argosy,* the first and most long-lived of the pulps, so pointedly explained: "The pulp magazine writers, the best of them, worked for markets that did not write for critics or attempt to satisfy timid advertisers. Not having to answer to anyone other than their readers, they wrote about human

♦ FOREWORD ♦

beings on the edges of the unknown, in those new lands the future would explore. They wrote for what we would become, not for what we had already been."

Some of the more lasting names that graced the pulps include H. P. Lovecraft, Edgar Rice Burroughs, Robert E. Howard, Max Brand, Louis L'Amour, Elmore Leonard, Dashiell Hammett, Raymond Chandler, Erle Stanley Gardner, John D. MacDonald, Ray Bradbury, Isaac Asimov, Robert Heinlein—and, of course, L. Ron Hubbard.

In a word, he was among the most prolific and popular writers of the era. He was also the most enduring—hence this series—and certainly among the most legendary. It all began only months after he first tried his hand at fiction, with L. Ron Hubbard tales appearing in *Thrilling Adventures, Argosy, Five-Novels Monthly, Detective Fiction Weekly, Top-Notch, Texas Ranger, War Birds, Western Stories,* even *Romantic Range.* He could write on any subject, in any genre, from jungle explorers to deep-sea divers, from G-men and gangsters, cowboys and flying aces to mountain climbers, hard-boiled detectives and spies. But he really began to shine when he turned his talent to science fiction and fantasy of which he authored nearly fifty novels or novelettes to forever change the shape of those genres.

Following in the tradition of such famed authors as Herman Melville, Mark Twain, Jack London and Ernest Hemingway, Ron Hubbard actually lived adventures that his own characters would have admired—as an ethnologist among primitive tribes, as prospector and engineer in hostile

• FOREWORD •

climes, as a captain of vessels on four oceans. He even wrote a series of articles for *Argosy,* called "Hell Job," in which he lived and told of the most dangerous professions a man could put his hand to.

Finally, and just for good measure, he was also an accomplished photographer, artist, filmmaker, musician and educator. But he was first and foremost a *writer,* and that's the L. Ron Hubbard we come to know through the pages of this volume.

This library of Stories from the Golden Age presents the best of L. Ron Hubbard's fiction from the heyday of storytelling, the Golden Age of the pulp magazines. In these eighty volumes, readers are treated to a full banquet of 153 stories, a kaleidoscope of tales representing every imaginable genre: science fiction, fantasy, western, mystery, thriller, horror, even romance—action of all kinds and in all places.

Because the pulps themselves were printed on such inexpensive paper with high acid content, issues were not meant to endure. As the years go by, the original issues of every pulp from *Argosy* through *Zeppelin Stories* continue crumbling into brittle, brown dust. This library preserves the L. Ron Hubbard tales from that era, presented with a distinctive look that brings back the nostalgic flavor of those times.

L. Ron Hubbard's Stories from the Golden Age has something for every taste, every reader. These tales will return you to a time when fiction was good clean entertainment and

• FOREWORD •

the most fun a kid could have on a rainy afternoon or the best thing an adult could enjoy after a long day at work.

Pick up a volume, and remember what reading is supposed to be all about. Remember curling up with a *great story*.

—Kevin J. Anderson

KEVIN J. ANDERSON *is the author of more than ninety critically acclaimed works of speculative fiction, including* The Saga of Seven Suns, *the continuation of the Dune Chronicles with Brian Herbert, and his* New York Times *bestselling novelization of L. Ron Hubbard's* Ai! Pedrito!

The Bold Dare All

CHAPTER ONE

Defiance to Timba's Ruler

THE sinuous length of the blacksnake whip threshed like a snake in agony upon the blazing coral sand.

Back and forth, back and forth, it left a crazy pattern of arcs and wiped out the prints of naked feet.

Eyes followed the lash, back and forth, as though the whip really was a snake with the powers of hypnotism.

High above the tatterdemalion crowd the spinning sun whipped down its quivers of molten arrows.

Palm fronds drooped in the windless heat. Where the sea plumed up from the outer reef rose lazy, rainbowed steam. Beyond lay the Celebes Sea, a glazed, heat-polished metallic sheet of scorching blue.

Inland loomed the mountains. Festering green tangles spread over the rough and jagged slopes like scum left by a receding tide.

The miserable huts along the shore crouched among the crawling vines, trying to hide their scaly thatch and blistered boards. From the horizon to the peaks, everything was harsh, brutal and ugly.

The men who stood in awful fascination were clad in tatters or not clad at all. Upon their gaunt and wasted features were stamped the hard-living histories of their lives.

Like the bleached bones of the sailing ship which rotted upon the coral sand, these men had been cast up by the sea and the sea did not want them back.

No one wanted them but Schwenk, and Schwenk wanted nothing but their physical abilities. He wanted their hands and their backs and he took them and broke them as he pleased. Schwenk needed them because he needed copra.

The blacksnake whip was still lashing, making a hissing sound as it moved. A hand, copper-plated by the sun, horny with work, battered with fighting, gripped the leather-sewn butt. The nails were dirty; the back of the hand was hairy.

Above the thick forearm clung a sweat-grimed sleeve. The throat of the shirt was ripped back, exposing a long, livid scar which was the handiwork of a certain native who had gone mad.

A native would have to be mad to attack Schwenk. This one was long ago cured of his mental disease. Buried to the ears in sand, honey smeared over his features, he had been abandoned to a tribe of ants who had mandibles sharp enough to go through ironwood.

Everyone was watching that whip. Schwenk's gloating eyes caressed the writhing length, up and down, up and down, measuring it with a blood-freezing expertness born of long, long practice.

Schwenk thrust his black tongue between his broken black teeth and moistened his lipless mouth. The bloated circle of his face lighted up. His flawless blue, bitterly cold killer eyes shifted suddenly to the back of the man.

The native moaned helplessly. His brown eyes were still on that moving lash. His hands were suspended high over his head, wrists lashed together, making his back muscles bulge beneath the chocolate-colored satin of his skin. He shivered.

Schwenk dug his heels into the white sand. He bent his body forward, dragged the lash back to its full ten feet of length.

Sssst! Crack!

Blood burbled up through the torn flesh and glistened in the sunlight.

Sssst! Crack!

The man screamed.

Sssst! Crack!

The crisscross pattern grew more complex and then began to blur. In a matter of seconds chunks of flesh were squared out and turned around and left dangling by small bits of skin.

It was impossible to see any pattern now. Only a dripping, red mass. Flies were swarming in upon it, leaping up and out of the way each time the whip struck, settling back when the lash drew away.

The natives in the crowd were staring and shaking. The two dozen white derelicts looked on unaffected.

But on the edge of the throng stood a man apart. He was not watching the lash. He was watching Schwenk with disdainful eyes, studying the hot satisfaction which blazed upon Schwenk's face at each crack of the whip.

Lee Briscoe had only been on Timba for two months. He had not yet had time to become a ragged scarecrow. He still pipe-clayed his helmet, he still polished his well-cut boots, he was still particular about the way his khaki breeches and shirts were starched.

The crowd knew nothing about him but they whispered that he was wanted by the law. No man would work for Schwenk of his own free will. Others held that Lee Briscoe had been an Army lieutenant and had murdered a soldier. But not one held the real clue as to why the man had chosen hellhole Timba for a retreat.

Lee Briscoe's eyes were clear and gray. His face was darkly burned. His cheekbones were high and prominent and his jaw was lean and firm. He was built wide at the shoulders and tapered off from there like a boxer.

Schwenk was beginning to sweat at his work, but that did not curtail his enjoyment of it in the least. He was just getting into good form when Lee Briscoe stepped into the clear space behind him and snatched the lash as it swung back.

Lee Briscoe threw the blacksnake thirty feet down toward the water, but he did not watch it go as the others did. He was looking straight at Schwenk.

Schwenk turned slowly. He looked at the tips of Briscoe's boots and then at the crown of Briscoe's helmet. Casually, not in the least excited, Schwenk put his hand on the heavy butt of his belted revolver.

"You got anything to say about it?" said Schwenk, carelessly. "Maybe you just forgot yourself. Maybe somebody told you I liked to be interrupted. That it?"

Lee Briscoe's words came slowly, with a drawl. "There isn't any reason to kill him. Finky was a good man."

"He's a thief," said Schwenk. "I've got five hundred natives on Timba. If they start stealing . . ."

"Finky wouldn't have stolen anything if you'd feed good rations. He was hungry. All he took was a can of salmon and a half-dozen biscuits. If he'd killed his partner, you wouldn't have had a word to say. That isn't justice, Schwenk."

Schwenk sneered at Briscoe, turned and barked at the men: "He's taking over the island, boys. Tip your hats to him. I said, tip your hats!"

Uneasily, the two dozen derelicts touched their fingers to their battered helmets and straws.

Schwenk faced Briscoe again, lipless mouth curling into a ghastly grin. "Now is there anything else you want, Briscoe? Maybe a Scotch and soda? WONG! Bring Briscoe a Scotch and soda!"

There came a full minute's silence and then Wong, opium-drugged, slant-eyed servant to Schwenk, came forth with the order on a tray.

"Drink it up," said Schwenk, hand on the butt of his gun. "Drink it up, Mr. Briscoe, because that's the last time you're ever going to drink anything on this earth. I'm going to murder you, Briscoe. Right here. And murder isn't pleasant. Here, don't mind me, drink up!"

Briscoe looked levelly at Schwenk and knew that the man meant every word he said. No man but Schwenk could carry a gun on Timba—except when the natives staged one of their frequent revolts.

Briscoe looked at the lacerated back of the unconscious

Finky. He told himself that it was worth it. He reached for the bottle and poured out a big slug of Scotch. Behind him, the derelicts moved out of the line of fire.

"To your health, Schwenk," said Briscoe, carelessly, seeming to look only at his glass.

Suddenly the amber fluid sloshed straight out. The alcohol stabbed into Schwenk's killer eyes.

With a yowl of agony, Schwenk lurched back. Briscoe's quick fingers plucked the gun from its holster and threw it after the whip.

Clawing at his face, Schwenk screamed a torrent of filthy abuse. In a moment he could see, in another moment he was trying to get his gun.

Briscoe rocked him with a mighty left, followed it with a right.

They went down into a swirl of sand, gouging, yelling, fighting with nails and boots and teeth.

A hoarse whistle raised the echoes of the jagged hills. The derelicts faced seaward and stared at the small steamer which was poking its nose into the lagoon.

It was one of Schwenk's six ships which served the better part of the Flores Sea, carrying freight, sometimes passengers, but chiefly copra.

Schwenk heard it, and although his mouth was full of sand and Briscoe's fist, he roared to his men for help.

They dared not refuse, those derelicts. They pulled Briscoe off and held him struggling while Schwenk retrieved his gun. They supposed of course that Schwenk would shoot

Briscoe immediately and have done with it. Instead, Schwenk holstered his weapon, spat out sand and said:

"Well, well, Mr. Briscoe. So you're a fighter, are you? We'll have to see some more about this later. Right now, let him go. Mr. Briscoe, you have the doubtlessly honorable privilege of being the first man under me who ever dared question my authority. That is very unique. If such a man were to behave himself, perhaps I could better use him. How about it?"

"You want my word or something of the sort?" said Briscoe.

"Your word?" shouted Schwenk with a laugh. "What good is that? I have a gun. That's enough for me. I'll break you, Briscoe, and I'll enjoy myself doing it. Shooting is too easy. Let him go."

The steamer was pulling alongside the wharf. On the bridge, gnarled and evil Captain Gunarson was yelling for somebody to catch his monkey fists. The crowd shuffled down to the sheet-iron warehouse and stood gaping up at the steamer deck.

Schwenk stopped in mid-pace and looked at the people on the deck. He let out a joyous curse, straightened his shirt, adjusted his helmet and permitted himself what he thought was a winning smile.

Briscoe had also stopped to stare.

There were a few native women on the island, of course. Some of the men had been fortunate enough to have had their wives brought into captivity with them.

But never before in the history of Timba had a white woman touched those harsh shores.

Briscoe frowned and looked uneasily at Schwenk's hurrying back. Briscoe looked up at the deck of the schooner again.

No, his eyes weren't lying to him. A girl was standing amid a tumble of baggage upon the deck. Coolly beautiful, in her turn she was looking at the motley crowd.

Briscoe felt something happen inside his chest.

She was dressed in the crispest white imaginable. She had a sweet, interesting face. She had a frank pair of eyes, utterly unafraid.

Beside her stood an elderly man, well dressed but somehow weak.

The man waved to Schwenk and Schwenk waved back. But Schwenk was staring only at the woman.

The gangway was down. The girl was coming carefully off. Schwenk was there to take her arm.

"Briscoe!" yelled Schwenk. "Take the lady's bags up to the house."

Briscoe was looking straight into the girl's eyes. He recovered himself with a jolt and faced Schwenk. "I've got something else to do."

He strode quickly up the beach and through the screening palms. He took a machete from a black man and cut the still-unconscious Finky down.

Giving Finky's feet into the care of a giant named Joffo and carrying the bloody head himself, Briscoe approached the mean, filthy thatched huts which made up the slave quarters.

"Doc" Rengarte, a drunken and disgraced French Army vet, tagged after them, combing the lice thoughtfully out of his gray beard.

"See that he gets well," ordered Lee Briscoe.

"You can't kill 'em," said Rengarte. "When I was in *le Maroc* I once had to operate—"

"If he dies," said Lee Briscoe, "you're liable to be tagging right after him."

"You're so emphatic, Briscoe. By the way, did you see that dame? Ah, quite lovely. And how you stared, Briscoe! Don't let Schwenk see you staring like that. He's got first rights around here, whether you admit it or not. . . . Ah, well, Briscoe, I suppose you'll have to kill me. This man's very, very dead."

CHAPTER TWO

Mike, Banjo and Tim, Conspirators

IT was something of a joke on Timba that Lee Briscoe washed and changed his clothes before the evening meal, but no one laughed openly about it anymore, not since a man named Hagger had been carried away from a slight altercation, which had been the result of such badgering.

Lee Briscoe's fists had become very respected things after that.

In a separate hut the natives had built for him, Briscoe was completing his evening cleanup. He had just finished lacing his artillery boots on the side when Mike Goddard thrust his shaggy, unkempt head inside the door.

"Old Swiney wants you right away," said Mike.

Briscoe looked up and acknowledged the message with a nod which also contained dismissal. But Mike Goddard had something else to say.

"You're sure hellbent on suicide, Lee. It's a wonder that old crackpot didn't drill you then and there."

"He's short of men," said Briscoe.

"Nuts. That ain't it at all. He knows killing you wouldn't cure you. He's going to have a lot of fun with you before he bumps you off."

"What makes you think that?"

"Oh, I dunno. It's his way, that's all. He's had men

kowtowing to him for so long, he's tired of it. And he's so damned sure of himself, he don't even consider it's dangerous keeping you around."

"Not very flattering, is it?" commented Briscoe, shrugging into a white jacket.

Mike scratched his nose, looked through the darkness to make certain they were alone, scratched his ribs uncertainly and, with several coughs, said, "If you ever figure on wiping this place up, Briscoe, me and Banjo Edwards and Tim Sullivan would kind of like to tag along. We've . . . we've got our bellyful of Schwenk."

"What could I do?" said Briscoe, carelessly lighting a cigarette.

"I was right behind you last week when those natives went screwy down Zaga River way. You ain't afraid of nothin', Lee. Banjo . . . well, he used to be a pretty good hand at picking locks in Sydney and he's got an impression of the keyholes in the gun shed. There's a submachine gun and a couple cases of rifles—"

"Sure you aren't talking to the wrong man?" said Briscoe.

Mike grinned and scratched his head. "You ain't got any love for Schwenk, Lee. And you didn't run out of civilization for picking somebody's pocket either. A guy like you could do a lot if he wanted to. These natives would follow you to hell and back, and me and Banjo Edwards and Tim Sullivan thought—"

"That isn't very healthy around here," said Briscoe.

"Listen, Lee, you don't know what that old son has got in his safe. Banjo could open it like it was paper. There's gold and bank notes and a whole bag of pearls. He ain't runnin' this copra business for his health, you know. In ten years he's taken out more than three million dollars. He blackbirds his own black ivory. He keeps us guys here because we're afraid of him. He makes other owners on other islands pay for his transportation costs. The only overhead he's got is grease for the Dutch and maybe a payoff for some bird like this one that just showed up. You think plenty about it, Lee."

"You said Schwenk wanted to see me?"

"Yeah."

"I'm on my way," said Briscoe, striding off into the dark.

Josef Schwenk's big house crouched on a hill overlooking the lagoon. Leading up to it in a wide curve was a white roadway flanked with royal palms, a gleaming ribbon in the dusk.

The house itself was built of coral rock, heavy and squatty like its owner, presenting a stark, brutal front to the world. The sea raked the rocks below it with white phosphorescent fingers which dug into the grottoes and blowholes, making weird and mournful sounds, giving rise to the native belief that the place was haunted.

But Schwenk was the only evil spirit living there. He had, said the natives, driven all the other devils away.

A tunnel led underground from the house to the grottoes by the sea, a means of escape in case a concerted revolt was staged by the natives. So far only a few at a time had attempted to murder Schwenk, but the Prussian lived in constant apprehension of the day when a united uprising would wipe out everything he had. Hence, the tunnel.

Lee Briscoe saw that the place was lighted up more than usual this night in honor of the guests. He paused to study it, and then to look down at his clothing. He saw that a lace was not well fastened on the side of his left boot. To remedy it, he moved to a curb in the shadow of a bush under the porch rail and bent to tidy the loose ends.

He had no more than leaned down when he heard footsteps at the other end of the veranda. Schwenk and the stranger were walking in his direction.

Knowing Schwenk's disposition, Briscoe stayed down. If Schwenk thought that he had been eavesdropping . . .

"He's coming up in a few minutes," growled Schwenk. "The reason I've gotten along in this world, Martin, is because I anticipate difficulties before they happen."

"Ah, and how you *have* gotten along!" replied Martin. "A big jump, *Herr* Schwenk, from *Oberleutnant Kommandant* of a microscopic post in German East Africa. Those English fools did you a favor when they ran you out, eh?"

"Keep a civil tongue in your face, Martin," said Schwenk. "You forget I was decorated with the Iron Cross of the First Class for devising those ambushes."

"Do not be so mighty, Schwenk. You have also forgotten that I was rewarded in a like manner for my spy work in Australia. It is Captain Wilhelm Martz, after all."

"The devil with that. What did you say the girl said?"

"She noticed your fine renegade and wanted very much to know who he was."

"Spotted Briscoe, did she? My strategy will take care of that."

• THE BOLD DARE ALL •

"Certainly," said Martin. "Have him shot or buried up to his neck or—"

"Really, Captain, you are very obvious. Pay heed to this. Lee Briscoe has been here but two months. I do not know where he came from. I was a fool to take him in at all. But he had a familiar look about him . . . but never mind, that was my mistake. I needed a white man and I hired Briscoe. Now, in two months, my dear Captain, he has caught the liking of the natives. They think he is a great man. Bah, little does he know about discipline. The lash is the only thing for discipline. But never mind. They like him. Just today he objected to a well deserved flogging I was handing out. I wanted to shoot him. God, how I wanted to blow his guts through his spine! But did I dare? No. Those natives were standing back there looking at me. I cannot kill this Briscoe like that, no matter how necessary it is. All the more necessary now that the girl has asked after him. He's a handsome fool, that Briscoe. Lives like a saint. Enough to turn any girl's head. Well, Captain, no wife of mine can have a thought for another man."

"Oh, I can handle that, *Herr* Schwenk. I can tell her—"

"Lily-livered methods don't go here. You think I go to all this trouble and expense to have this woman look at another man? You are a great fool, Captain, if you think that. No, she would not look at these other derelicts, of course. But Briscoe . . . !"

"But all you have to do is kill this Briscoe . . ."

"And have the natives revolt? No, Captain, I have not taken

all the money out of Timba that I can take out. I do not intend to wreck carefully laid plans. Now, attend me. You are satisfied with the fifty thousand dollars I have promised you?"

"Of course. The girl is nothing to me. I little thought when I sent you that picture of her..."

"A man gets lonely in such a place, Captain. The picture did not do her justice. She is cheap at fifty thousand. If we remove every cause for trouble she may consent to marrying me. If she refuses then, we still have other ways, eh?"

"Then what will you do about Briscoe?"

Schwenk laughed.

"I discredit him to the girl. I make him chief overseer and then discredit him to the natives. Finally, when he has not a single friend left, I kill him. It is a good plan, eh?"

"Excellent."

"See what happens to him, my friend. He will be glad to die when I have finished with him. There are many subtle ways, Captain, which even a wonder at sabotage like yourself cannot touch for brilliance. You get your fifty thousand, I get this woman. Everyone is satisfied. . . . I wonder what the devil is detaining that Briscoe. Come in and have a drink while we wait."

They disappeared into the house and Briscoe was able to stand up straight.

For the space of a minute he stood staring into the lighted doorway. A bitter smile came to his lips and then faded when he thought about this beast Schwenk marrying a girl like that.

He went back down the road as silently as a shadow. Then, turning, he walked loudly up the drive and up the steps.

Schwenk stepped out on the porch. He was quite at ease, even smiling.

The light struck Briscoe's face.

Involuntarily, Schwenk stepped back and dropped his hand to a concealed holster. Instantly recovering his poise and his humorless grin, Schwenk gave Briscoe a mock bow.

"All dressed for dinner, Briscoe. Come in, come in, we've been waiting." In a low undertone, he added, "You'll be on your good behavior. I'll have no rows tonight."

Briscoe nodded impassively and let Schwenk enter first. Quite as if dining with Timba's overlord was a matter of little moment to him, he walked across the veranda and into the wide hall.

Blear-eyed Wong looked at him distrustfully and shuffled out of sight into the kitchen.

Schwenk thrust his guest forward and into the dining room.

The girl and the strange man were already there. The table was set with crystal and brilliant silver. Tall candles were burning, shedding a yellow luster upon the bright, stiff linen.

"Miss Martin, this is my new manager, Lee Briscoe. Martin, Briscoe."

Calmly, not in the least moved by the sudden elevation in rank, Briscoe bowed slightly over the girl's hand and shook the limp fingers of her evident father.

"Briscoe," said Schwenk, fixing his cold, killer eyes upon Briscoe's lean face, "saved my life this afternoon. I am most liberal with rewards when men's actions please me."

"How interesting," said the girl, looking at Briscoe with frank interest. "How did it happen?"

"I was half-dead with boredom," said Schwenk, lids dropping halfway down. "I objected to a little flirtation he was having with a native woman and he tried to kill me. I like men with spirit, eh, Briscoe?"

The girl looked away as though ashamed of the friendliness she had displayed a moment before.

Martin laughed in a wheezy way. "Josef, you always were a most amusing fellow."

Briscoe broadsided Schwenk with a rage-filled glance, but he was unwilling to make a scene in front of the girl. He knew instantly why Schwenk had brought him there.

Schwenk had seen Briscoe's look on the dock and, with true strategy, was averting any possible friendship which might damage his own case with the girl.

"Sit down," said Schwenk, pulling back the girl's chair. "Briscoe, be on your good behavior tonight. Remember we have company. He has a way about him, Miss Martin. A devil with the ladies, but sometimes rather crude, eh, Briscoe? Men get that way when they are in constant association with races other than their own."

Briscoe took himself in hand. Obviously, Schwenk expected him to bite back. If Schwenk wanted that, it would not happen. Briscoe took his place across from Miss Martin.

Dinner was begun in uncomfortable silence, but soon Martin began to drag Schwenk into conversation.

"Those were the days," said Martin, with a flabby smile. "It was *German* East Africa then. You were the best commandant in the district, Josef. Ah, how those devils stepped when you barked at them! That's what they need. An iron hand!

Discipline is good for them. A man can't maintain any control over the natives unless he has the right to flog. You always said that, Josef. Tell me, how did you get such a wonderful island as this all to yourself? It must be very large."

"About two hundred square miles," said Schwenk.

"How did you get it?" persisted Martin.

"I procured it from a chap named Fremont," said Schwenk.

The girl had been watching Briscoe with puzzled eyes. She saw something like a smile flit across his mouth and disappear when Schwenk said that and she expected Briscoe to voice the remark which was obviously on the tip of his tongue. But he went on eating.

Schwenk crammed a large forkful of meat into his mouth and chewed it with great relish, gazing upon Miss Martin with undisguised admiration as though about to take a forkful of her.

"Tell me, Martin," said Schwenk, "how is it that you came by such a lovely daughter? You weren't even married when I last saw you and that was but fifteen years ago, while this young lady is at least twenty."

"She was my wife's girl," said Martin. "My wife was married to an Australian officer who got killed in the war, you know. She died a year after we were married and I've raised Diana as she wanted me to. The best schools, the best clothes. Diana goes everywhere with me now. I missed her a great deal while she was with her mother's people in San Francisco."

"I imagine you did," said Schwenk. "But we'll show her a good time here. Of course, you know, she'll have to be very careful never to go out unescorted. The natives, you know, are restless, and Briscoe and the rest of the riffraff on the island are never to be trusted, eh, Briscoe?"

"Never," said Briscoe, as definitely as though he held a revolver in each hand and had just finished shooting Schwenk dead.

"It is very hard," said Schwenk, "to live like a gentleman in such a place. But I manage to get along."

"I should think it would be dangerous," said Diana Martin.

"Oh, they try to kill me quite frequently, in spite of all I've done for them," said Schwenk. "Why, just this afternoon, when I found him with that woman . . . but then I've already told you about Briscoe, haven't I?"

"Already," said Briscoe.

"But, Miss Diana," said Schwenk, "you mustn't get the wrong idea of my overseer-in-chief. He's really quite a splendid fellow. You were in the Army, weren't you, Briscoe? That is, before you bayoneted that sergeant . . . or was it a sergeant?"

"A sergeant," said Briscoe, helpfully, small devils in his eyes. "I killed him because he kept telling lies about me. He was about five feet ten inches tall and he had grayish hair and hardly any lips and a very cold pair of eyes and big hands and he talked with a slight German accent."

"Why," said Martin in surprise, "he must have looked very like Josef."

"That's so," said Briscoe, as though astonished about it. "Just like Josef Schwenk."

Diana Martin caught the edge of madness in Briscoe's voice and she braced herself for a sudden, swift outburst.

"This sergeant," said Briscoe, "was very conceited and boorish. He made the mistake of underestimating everyone about him. But one night he aimed too high. He tried to make love to a girl a thousand times too good for him. I told him not to go on with the affair. I gave him ample warning. I told him to let the girl alone and stick to beating soldiers. But he would never listen to anyone. He had already made the mistake of taking something which did not belong to him, and when he was about to steal this girl as well and when he refused to listen to reason, I went into his tent one night and I took a bayonet and I stuck it squarely between the third and fourth ribs."

"What a ghastly story," gaped Martin, completely missing the point. "And then you ran away, of course."

"No," said Briscoe.

"But how . . . why? . . ." said Martin.

"They gave me a medal for it," said Briscoe.

Schwenk was amused. He laughed loudly and delightedly. "You're a great one, Briscoe. This is certainly a streak of luck, having somebody here to entertain my guests. You must pardon him, Miss Diana. He's really quite a good fellow. Of course, when he is drunk he is rather bad, but you're not always drunk, are you, Briscoe? By the way, you had better go down to the stables tonight and tell them to have a couple horses ready in the morning."

"Now?" said Briscoe.

"Yes, now. Martin is here to look after that blight that's been hitting along the Zaga bottoms. Can't have the crop injured, you know."

Briscoe stood up and went to the door.

Schwenk called, "And leave that native woman alone, Briscoe. I won't have you getting drunk and making a fool of yourself while Miss Diana is here."

"Good night," said Briscoe with an easy smile.

The girl did not answer him. She did not even look at him. Her eyes were cast down and she had a disappointed air about her.

Briscoe tramped down the curving road by the light of a new moon. He went straight to the stables and relayed Schwenk's orders. Then he rapped upon a thatched hut nearby and stood with his back to the door.

Shaggy Mike Goddard shuffled forth. A moment later Tim Sullivan came out, followed by Banjo Edwards.

Briscoe led off toward a dark clump of bamboo trees. The three single-filed after him.

Tim Sullivan, lanky, awkward and ever morose, nudged Banjo Edwards. Banjo had a face like a full moon, white as lard, in which two round eyes sat in permanent amazement. Banjo grinned in a satisfied manner.

Briscoe stopped, slowly applied a match to a smoke and looked carefully at the three before him.

"You fellows want to start something?" said Briscoe.

"I already told you, Lee," said Mike, scratching his stomach.

"You remember what he did to Stoddard?"

"Hung him," said Tim, creakily. "Just like he'll probably hang us."

"You think after what happened on the Zaga that any of the natives will stand in with me?" said Briscoe.

"Sure, Lee. You been helping them with food and medicine," said Banjo.

"How long do you think we could hold out if he called in a Dutch gunboat?" said Briscoe.

"Not very long," said Tim, gloomily. "The only reason you're throwing in with us is because of that girl."

"Maybe," said Briscoe. "What of it?"

"Nothin'," said Tim. "If you ain't got anything against sudden death, we ain't neither."

"Worse livin' here than dyin'," said Mike.

"What can you do, Mike?" said Briscoe.

"I was a pretty good steam engineer once," said Mike.

"And you, Banjo?" said Briscoe.

"Ain't any lock made I can't pick. Ain't any safe ever built I can't crack. And I was a sailor once. I used to be a pretty good machinist, but that was before I took to studying photography so I could counterfeit five-pound notes. Then of course there's the time I was in the French Army as a cook. Come to think of it, I was a steeplejack about twenty years ago. That was before I—"

"Plenty," said Briscoe. "And you, Sullivan?"

"I never amounted to much, I guess," said Sullivan, "but I could navigate a boat pretty well if I didn't run it on the rocks or something or get sunk by a typhoon or—"

"Looks like it's the sea," said Briscoe. "When does that steamer leave here?"

"Schwenk won't send it for another ten days," said Mike. "We can throw that old devil Gunarson to the sharks and knife those Kanakas and—"

"You let me do the planning," said Briscoe. "In the meantime, look dumb and stay dumb. I'll pick the natives."

"We'll probably get drunk and talk," gloomed Sullivan. "Or somebody may spill it to Old Swiney. He'd string us all up if he couldn't think of anything worse. He keeps a machine gun in his bedroom and I wouldn't be surprised if he turned it on us the next time we get near...."

"And outside of all of us dropping dead from heart failure," said Briscoe, "everything's fine. Good night, gentlemen."

CHAPTER THREE

Threat and Counter-Threat

TWO days passed before Briscoe again had a chance to see Diana Martin. He had not been invited to the house again, and his new duties as overseer-in-chief of Timba made him range from the murky Zaga River to the lowering, sweltering Madina Range.

Late in the afternoon he had come upon Mike's workmen in a ravine several miles from the house. The natives were engaged in the work of hulling out coconut meat for drying and the only sound was the whack of the machetes. Mike was lounging in the shade. He started up guiltily when he heard the hoofbeats of a horse, but he sank down again when he saw that it was Briscoe.

"Getting along all right?" said Briscoe.

"Sure," said Mike, scratching between his shoulder blades. "Since you took over, things have been pretty quiet. Old Swiney is hanging around the house. If things would only stay this way, Lee, I'd be satisfied. But they won't. Not a bit of it. That dame is going to spell trouble sooner or later, and you ain't going to last very long or I lose my bet."

"Bet?" said Briscoe.

"Sure, we got a pool on it. If you last until the first of next month, Tim wins. If you last to the fifteenth, I win. If you last until the twentieth, Rengarte wins. And if it goes clear to the fifteenth of the next, we donate the money to the rum fund. But it won't never be donated. We'll clear—"

"Watch yourself," cautioned Briscoe, listening.

Another horse was coming down the twilight jungle trail. Coming fast.

Mike scrambled up and went to work. The natives began to move nervously about. It might be Schwenk and Schwenk had been known to shoot a man for loafing.

But it was not Old Swiney. It was Diana Martin.

She came down into the ravine and had started up before she saw the motionless Briscoe. He was blocking her trail and though he had started to move aside for her, the quick look she gave him and the way she searched with her eyes on either side of him for a way to get by made him stay where he was.

Diana was game. She reined in, sat easily in her saddle and gave Briscoe a white smile.

"No need to be afraid of me," said Briscoe.

"Why . . . why, don't be foolish. I'm not afraid . . . of you."

He knew then that she was afraid of him. Very much afraid. Her small hand on the reins shook a little and she met his eyes with an effort, dropping her own every few seconds to find a way past him.

"You've been listening to Schwenk," said Briscoe.

"I . . . I don't know what you're talking about, Mr. Briscoe."

"You've been hearing that I'm pretty much of a devil one way and another. You'll keep on hearing it right up to the day you and Schwenk get married."

"Oh, but I'm not going to marry him."

"Oh, but yes, you are, whether you know it or not. You came here to marry him."

"Really, Mr. Briscoe, I must be going. They didn't see me leave and if I fail to return right away, they'll miss me and search. I just came out for a short ride. It's a lovely island, isn't it?"

Mike Goddard was standing at her stirrup. He laughed suddenly. She gave a start, not having seen him come up on her. She tugged at the reins restlessly and looked behind her. The half-naked natives had all stopped work. Their eyes were fixed upon her. She felt trapped.

It was hardly a time for polite conversation, but Briscoe did not know when he would get another chance.

"If you ever need help," he said simply, "I'll be on call."

"Thank you . . . but I hardly think that that will be necessary. Mr. Schwenk is very kind . . ."

Mike let out another bellow of amusement and the horse shied.

"Let me by," ordered Diana.

Courteously, Briscoe drew out of her way. She was too anxious to be gone and she laid on sharply with her quirt. The horse snorted and reared and almost threw her.

Instinctively, Briscoe reached out and snatched at her waist, pulling her from the saddle before she could fall.

For the space of ten seconds she clung to him. Then, suddenly, she realized where she was and who Briscoe was and began to struggle.

He tried to let her down while Mike got her horse, but

Diana had heard a great deal about Briscoe, all of it bad, and she failed to understand that his motive was purely gallant.

Twisting about she raised her quirt and tried to strike him.

Briscoe dodged and she would have fallen again if he had not gripped her tightly.

It suited Schwenk's character perfectly that he would choose that moment to announce himself.

He had evidently been sitting still on the brink of the ravine after following the girl's horse along the muddy jungle trail.

Now he dug in his spurs, yelled and came down the ravine riding hard. In an instant he whipped Diana out of Briscoe's grasp and quickly deposited her on the ground. In the next, Schwenk drew his revolver and aimed it at Briscoe's chest.

"The instant my back is turned," roared Schwenk, "you try your devilish tricks with the only decent woman you ever met! Damn you, Briscoe, I'll blow you—"

Briscoe dodged, lashed out with his quirt and knocked down the gun. It fell from Schwenk's stinging hand toward the muck. But Mike was under it with lightning speed. He flipped the revolver up. Briscoe caught it, reversed it, and before Schwenk knew what had happened, he himself was covered.

"I don't want to get you this way, Schwenk," said Briscoe, "although it would be a pleasure. You have no idea, Schwenk, what a kick I'd get out of drilling you, and neither have you any idea of the numerous scores we'll someday settle. Right now, Schwenk, help the lady mount her horse and clear out of here before I change my mind."

"Damn you, Briscoe. Don't think you can get away with everything. There's a limit. Give me that gun."

"I need this gun. I also need that ammunition belt and holster. Mike, take the belt off him."

"Touch this belt and I'll—"

"You'll what?" mocked Briscoe. "You're a yellow pup, Schwenk. You won't do a thing to Mike. And you won't touch me. If you do, I'll have five hundred natives storming your house within the hour, whether I'm alive or dead. They'd string you up, soak you in gasoline and let you burn."

"The Dutch—" blustered Schwenk.

"Damn the Dutch. I can pay as much for protection as you can. Get out of here before I change my mind and blow you all over the landscape."

Diana had mounted. Seeing the trail clear before her, she rode swiftly up toward the jungle edge. Schwenk saw her go, looked uncertainly at the revolver in Briscoe's hand and then followed her.

"I've done it now," said Briscoe, ruefully buckling on the belt. "She thinks I'm a devil."

"I've known women to love devils," said Mike, thoughtfully scratching his leg.

"Not her kind."

"There's no difference in kind," said Mike.

Joffo, the gigantic Swahili, moved toward Briscoe like a panther. "Why you no killum? Them fellah boy like killum along you plenty. Why you no killum?"

"Think I want his murder on my hands?" said Briscoe.

"I killum along that fellah boy hog," said Joffo. "Givum along that pistol and I killum plenty for you."

"We'll wait a while," said Briscoe.

"Why wait? Allatime that fellah boy figure out to killum white boss. Killum fellah boy hog first time, number one."

"Ladies don't like murder," said Briscoe.

"What for not like killum? Funny gal no like killum. My gal like me one time when I got two heads on poles. Before that she no likum. What for this fellah missie different native gal?"

"You'll have your chance," promised Briscoe.

"Give it to them now," pleaded Mike. "Look here, in fifteen minutes I could get word to almost every native boy on Timba. They like you. They think you're a real chief-boss, Lee. Don't let that ugly devil get the best of you. He's up there loading that dame down with a lot of lies. Listen. You give me that pistol and I'll sneak up tonight and put it against the back of his neck and pull the trigger. You take the dame. I'll take those pearls and we'll light out."

"She wouldn't go for that," said Briscoe. "She thinks Schwenk is somebody."

"She wouldn't go for that!" mocked Mike, emphatically itching the small of his back. "I knew a swell little cookie down in Sydney once that wouldn't have nothin' to do with me until I bumped off Jigger Evans. She was his gal. She liked me because she figured I was the tougher gent, see? Women are all the same. She'll get sick of that Schwenk and she'll eat out her heart for you. I know women. She respects you. You got her scared. She figures you're the toughest gent on Timba. Don't be a sap. Walk in and take what you want. I'll kill Schwenk—"

"And have the Dutch hang the lot of us. They'd do it quick enough if anything happened to a gold mine like Schwenk. There are other ways, Mike. The *Sultan* is still in the harbor. We'll take the steamer and get away. If we don't bother Schwenk much, the Dutch won't even follow us. Let me handle this."

"All right," said Mike. "But tonight I'm going to bet ten guilders that you don't last forty-eight hours more."

CHAPTER FOUR

Schwenk's Answer to Rebels

BRISCOE lasted the forty-eight hours. He lasted another twenty-four besides, but at the end of it, he was shaking with the strain of watching every bush ahead of him on the trail from which might come a fatal bullet.

But no bullet came. When he saw Schwenk, Schwenk was the height of courtesy, making no reference at all to the flagrant holster and gun butt which jutted away from Briscoe's well-tailored breeches.

Diana had evidently taken her encounter to heart. She was not to be seen away from the house, though Briscoe waited several times along the trail where she had ridden before.

The *Sultan* was still at the dock. Tim and Banjo and Mike were impatient to get going.

The four met in the afternoon in Briscoe's hut.

Briscoe quickly outlined the plan.

"I'm going through with this," said Briscoe, "because I'm certain that something else is afoot and I'm not at all certain but what my influence with the natives is being steadily undermined. You've filed out those keys to the gun room?"

"You bet," said Banjo, jingling them in his pocket.

"Good. You and Tim are to get the guns at dark. Mike is to wait on the dock. I'll make sure that Schwenk is nowhere in the vicinity when it happens. Somehow I'll get Diana away from the house. We will steal aboard the ship, knock out the three men on watch, tie up Gunarson, silently get up steam and then, before anything can happen to prevent us, we'll be out of the harbor."

"What about those pearls and the money?" said Mike.

"Banjo's lookout," said Briscoe.

"You mean you'll consent to us stealing them?" said Tim.

"I won't consent to you stealing them and if you take them you won't be stealing anything."

"A million bucks?" wheezed Banjo. "You don't think a million bucks is something?"

"You don't get me," said Briscoe. "But we'll let it pass as it is."

"We'll probably all get caught," said Tim. "If one of the sailors lets out a yip, Schwenk will turn a machine gun on the bridge and we won't have a chance."

"Want to back out?" said Briscoe, sharply.

"No, but the Dutch will probably hunt us down," said Tim, morosely. "If we go to Sydney, we'll get caught and we ain't got the fuel to go anyplace else."

"We won't go to Sydney," said Briscoe.

"If not Sydney, then where can we go?" whispered Banjo.

"We're not going very far. We're taking the *Sultan* so that we can pen Schwenk up on Timba. We nail his other five boats as they come in. We tie them up on Rossman Island across the channel. No radio here. No chance of the Dutch coming in. Schwenk can't send out word by canoe, can he?"

"No, but he'll find some way," muttered Tim.

"How can he?" demanded Briscoe. "We're going to paralyze

• THE BOLD DARE ALL •

Schwenk, drive him to terms, cut him off from the world and... well, I have another answer for it, too, but I can't give you that right now. In the meanwhile, have you got your jobs straight? At eight o'clock we meet on the edge of the dock."

"At eight," said Banjo.

"Schwenk will probably get there first," moaned Tim. "But I guess it's better than rotting on Timba forever. Why can't we just kill him and let it go at that, Lee?"

"No murder," said Briscoe. "That outlaws us."

"I suppose piracy won't," said Tim.

"Who'll find out about it?" demanded Briscoe.

"Schwenk," said Tim. "That's enough. If you'll just let me slip a knife into him, quiet-like—"

"At eight," said Briscoe, interrupting him.

"At eight," said Mike.

"At eight," sighed Tim, as though it was the date of his funeral.

It was not as hot as usual that night, the thermometer having dropped to a hundred and five. A wind was blowing in from the sea, bending the palm fronds and making them clatter like old bones shaken in a shroud.

Hatless, dressed in dark khaki, revolver swinging loosely at his hip, Briscoe approached the big house on the hill.

There were few lights there that night and no sign of anyone about the place. The gun shed, a sort of pillbox fort itself, was without a guard.

The gray, sharp walls made a lonely picture against the

cloud-interspersed stars. The sea in the grottoes moaned and whispered awful things—of murdered men and drowned sailors and tortured natives.

Briscoe stopped in the roadway and looked back at the flat below where the natives had built a leaping blaze. The squalid huts showed up in the flickering yellow light and looked less forlorn than they did by day. The weary natives moved slowly back and forth before the flames, hopeless, broken men.

Briscoe went up toward the house again. He did not know just what he would do or how he would get Diana out of the place or just how he could temporarily remove Schwenk, if at all.

According to his watch he had fifteen minutes before the appointed time. Fifteen minutes were enough if nothing untoward blocked him.

The absence of a guard surprised him. Lately Schwenk had taken to posting some renegade on the steps and another renegade in the shadows to watch the first, while Schwenk himself, from time to time, at unexpected moments, watched the second.

As everyone more or less watched Schwenk, the round was complete.

But tonight there was no guard.

In the open, Briscoe approached the steps. He stopped suddenly. Diana was sitting on the veranda, looking down the path. She must have seen him and yet she had given no sign of it.

Things could not have been better, Briscoe told himself. If

he could possibly get her to come peacefully, the deed was as good as done. But even if he had to gag and carry her away, the matter was still simple.

He slid into the shadows, rounded the end of the veranda, silently went over the rail. Diana was in profile to him. She seemed tense, ill at ease.

Briscoe slid along the rail, undecided about his tactics.

He had to get her away from there for her own good, no matter what she happened to think about it at the moment. He could take his time convincing her later. When she fully understood his position, she would realize that he had done her a favor.

From his pocket he took a clean handkerchief and three small lengths of rope. Rough it would have to be, there was no help for it.

"Hello, Briscoe," said Schwenk. "You're just in time. I was about to send down for you."

Briscoe relaxed, put the rope and handkerchief back in his pocket. His fingers itched to grab his revolver, but he knew by the tone of Schwenk's voice that he was amply covered.

A moment later, Briscoe's gun left its holster to be thrust in Schwenk's waistband.

Diana's white face was turned toward them. She was sitting back now, motionless, waiting.

"Turn around, Briscoe," said Schwenk, casually.

Briscoe turned. Schwenk had a .45 Derringer.

"Yes, Briscoe," said Schwenk, "I was about to send for you. Come along. We'll go down to the beach."

Diana said nothing. Her only move was to turn her head slightly as the two men rounded a curve in the roadway.

Briscoe tried to be airy about it.

"I didn't know hogs had such a keen sense of smell," said Briscoe.

"I didn't know," said Schwenk, "that a man who bathed as often as you do could stink so much."

"What's this to be?" said Briscoe. "A firing squad?"

"Guilty conscience?" said Schwenk.

"Deep insight," said Briscoe.

"I'm a deep man."

They entered the clearing before the slave houses. Schwenk had crossed his arms and no one could see the Derringer, though it was still there.

"You go first," said Schwenk, "so follow my orders."

"It's a pleasure," said Briscoe.

"I want the crew to my longboat," said Schwenk, loudly. "Lee Briscoe has some business up along Zaga way."

Six natives stepped out. Schwenk sent two of them back. The others walked down to the beach and thrust the longboat out into the lagoon.

Loudly Schwenk said, "Briscoe, you go up there and see about that blight. You'll be there in the morning. You stay upriver for a couple weeks. Get the supplies from Stephans at the Zaga post. When you've got all the blight mapped out, report back here."

"What's the gag?" said Briscoe in a low voice.

"That's fine. You've got it straight then," roared Schwenk. He added in a whisper, "Get into that boat. If you try to put back ashore, remember I've got a rifleman posted on the cliff up there."

Briscoe stepped over the gunwale and into the stern. When he took the tiller, the native boys ran out into the water and stepped, dripping, into their places. The longboat bobbed broadside to the beach. The boys lifted up their oars.

"Prepare to give way," said Briscoe. "Give way all together."

"And keep going," added a harsh voice from the pile of sail in the bow.

A .38 Colt gleamed in the starlight and behind it glittered the bright orbs of Captain Gunarson. Beside him lay a naked Kanaka hugging an Enfield rifle.

"Stroke," said Briscoe. "Stroke."

As though he had not heard a thing, he paced his rowing crew until they rounded a point and the fire disappeared from sight.

Gunarson sat up. He was a singularly ugly man. Twisted and bony, a slave to bad temper, he was greatly feared on Timba.

"Keep going, renegade," said Gunarson. "In a minute, start heading straight out to sea. When you get a mile from shore go south until you are off Schwenk's point. Then head in."

"Nicely planned," said Briscoe.

"You're damned right it is," snapped Gunarson, bringing the .38 to full cock. "Head out to sea."

The native boys knew that as long as they followed the orders of the man with the gun they were reasonably safe. They pulled strongly, bodies rippling with effort, glistening with sweat and spray.

Briscoe tucked the tiller post under his arm, got out a cigarette.

"None of that," growled Gunarson. "Think I want those natives to see you from shore?"

"I didn't think you did," said Briscoe with a sigh.

It took them about an hour to row the three sides of the quadrangle. They had passed the slave huts so far at sea the fire had been but a yellow dot in the ebony night.

The moon was coming up, turning the horizon into green gold. But it was too late to show up the longboat to the natives, and even if they had seen it they would not have understood.

Briscoe steered in toward the point. The hissing, boiling sea was battering itself into an angry fury against the pockmarked coral formation. At one place and one place only was it quiet. That was the entrance to a long and narrow passage a freshwater stream, combined with the sea, had eaten through the soft lime.

They steered into it. The motion of the water grew less and then ceased altogether.

Overhead the uneven roof grew higher. The echoes of the sea muttered fitfully against the rough walls.

Ahead a lantern glowed beside a natural landing stage. Briscoe steered the longboat up to it. The natives tossed their oars.

A Kanaka was holding the lantern. Beside him Schwenk was standing, lipless mouth curled into a triumphant leer.

"Hello, Briscoe," said Schwenk. "Back again so soon. Have a nice trip, Briscoe? Unload them, Gunarson. Briscoe will be wanting a slug of Scotch after his long ride."

Briscoe followed the boat's crew ashore. Gunarson and his businesslike Kanaka sailor were alert and watchful for any trouble, ready to fire on the instant.

They left the stage in single file, walking up a long incline which wound through great masses of white coral. Presently they were out of Schwenk's well-built tunnel and into a large, dark, airless chamber.

The feeble lantern rays did not reach far. They did not need to.

Securely bound, lying in a neat row, were Tim Sullivan, Mike Goddard and Banjo Edwards.

Briscoe looked at Schwenk and then beyond him. "Doc" Rengarte was standing there grinning. That, then, was the answer to all this. Rengarte had spied upon them, had listened to them, had reported their every move to Schwenk. When he saw the cold disdain, the bitter rage in Briscoe's glance, Rengarte stopped smiling and moved closer to Schwenk.

The boat's crew, although they had been no party to the attempted escape, only because they might talk, were tied up and chained to the wall.

Briscoe tried to keep them from braceleting his wrists, but they had him in a moment. Rusty iron clanked. Briscoe sat down against the cold rock.

"It won't be long, Briscoe," said Schwenk, pleasantly. "In three weeks, as soon as I am certain that the natives will make no connection between myself and your disappearance, you'll get right out of here. I promise it faithfully, Briscoe. Right down the incline and to the landing stage. At high tide, Briscoe, sharks come in there, you know."

"Sharks come in here, too," said Briscoe.

"Quite a wit, isn't he, Gunarson?" said Schwenk. "By the way, gentleman, I'll have a Kanaka guard posted outside, so just sit down here and get a good rest. *Auf Wiedersehen.*"

Rengarte, Schwenk and Gunarson left with the Kanakas. The eight in the chamber sat quietly after that, looking straight ahead, saying nothing.

"I knew it," said Tim, at last. "And them natives will forget all about you in three weeks. We're stuck, Lee."

CHAPTER FIVE

Men in Irons—

WHAT, Briscoe? Don't tell me you haven't shaved! And your clothes, Briscoe. So rumpled and dirty! And your face! Why, all week we've been feeding you up like a prize beef on bread and water and you haven't even the good grace to get fat about it."

Schwenk stood in the roughly hewn doorway of the cavern. His eyes were withdrawn into the fat folds of his face and his thin mouth was curved in a crooked, gloating grin.

Schwenk went on, "You'll have to pardon my discourtesy, Briscoe. I've been so very busy I really haven't had time to entertain you properly. But we'll remedy that very shortly. Very, very shortly, Briscoe. And how are the rest of your fine mutineers? Why, don't tell me they look seedy, too! Gentlemen, gentlemen, have you no pride of appearance whatever? Take your cue from Briscoe. See how neat and tidy he's kept himself!"

"Go away," muttered Briscoe. "Go away and drown yourself or something. Go take some cyanide."

Schwenk laughed and came forward in the dim, greenish light. He sat down on a coral stone, facing Briscoe, studying him, grinning.

Briscoe, after a week of hell, looked much the worse for wear.

*What, Briscoe? Don't tell me you haven't shaved!
And your clothes, Briscoe. So rumpled and dirty!*

• THE BOLD DARE ALL •

Sleeping on sharp stone, eating nothing but dry bread and drinking nothing but scummy water had caused his cheeks to sink in until his face was little more than the caricature of a skull. But if Briscoe looked bad, Mike, Banjo and Tim looked even worse. The natives did not appear as bad off. Indeed, they had hardly changed at all, due to the full ration brought them every day. It amused Schwenk to feed them well.

"I came down for a good purpose, Briscoe," said Schwenk. "You should be very flattered that I come to tell you the news first. I've told no one else, you know."

"Keep your news and go away. This place stinks enough now."

"You have a pretty way of expressing yourself, Briscoe. You make me hesitate about confiding in you. But then, I've always been very considerate of you, Briscoe, and I really wouldn't like to leave you ignorant of this affair."

"What affair?"

"Ah, you're interested now, eh? I wanted to tell you about Martin, Briscoe."

"What about Martin?"

Schwenk drew a long breath and sighed. "Poor chap. His creditors have sent word that they will be held off no longer. He must pay or go to jail, Briscoe. But of course I couldn't help him, even if he is an old friend."

"Sabotage didn't pay him well enough, that it?" said Briscoe, propping himself up against the stone and swinging his irons into a less weighty position.

"Sabotage?" spat Schwenk in a surprised voice. "How did you . . . What gave you such silly ideas, Briscoe?"

"You mean what gave you and Captain Martz such silly

ideas. Good God, Schwenk, do you think you can run the whole world?"

"Briscoe, you give me pause. You make me wonder about things. I've recently had all your baggage searched, old fellow. On a grip we found the initials L. F. On a binocular case we found the initials L. B. F. On a picture, Briscoe, we found L. F. I've been wondering what your real name might be. Not Fremont, perhaps?"

"It's hard to tell, isn't it?" said Briscoe.

"Not so hard. I also found a little magazine in your trunk, Briscoe. The Army and Navy Register. It said something about First Lieutenant L. B. Fremont being granted a year's leave of absence without pay."

"Is that so?" said Briscoe. "Why do you suppose an Army man would want a year's leave? Very strange, isn't it?"

"Not so strange. Both you and I know that a man named Fremont is buried up on that high ridge behind the slave houses. Died from fever, poor fellow."

"Well, you at least buried him."

"Of course. But I don't think I'll have to bury you, Briscoe. No, I don't think so. Sometime when you haven't anything better to do, hitch yourself down to the float at high tide and watch the sharks coming in through the reef. There's a big one down there. About thirty feet long, he is. A man could walk upright through his mouth, but of course I don't expect you to be walking about that time."

"Schwenk, you bore me."

"That's unfortunate, Briscoe. Why don't you get up and leave, eh? But none of this. Did I tell you about Martin?"

"Go ahead. I'll wait until you've finished."

"Thank you," said Schwenk. "The poor man is badly in debt—"

"You said that once. But fifty thousand dollars will get him out of debt, won't it?"

"Briscoe, you amaze me. That's the exact amount. However, I really couldn't give away fifty thousand dollars, you know."

"Of course not. So you are going to take the girl off his hands. Go on, Schwenk."

"Damn you!" yelled Schwenk, suddenly. "How did you find that out?"

"I know you and your ways, that's all. Calm yourself, Schwenk, and pray continue. I won't interrupt."

Schwenk was silent for a long time. Finally he went on. "I knew what you were going to do. You knew what I was going to do. You've lost. Diana thinks a great deal of her father. She's willing to save him by marrying me. I came down here to tell you just this: Tomorrow night, if you listen hard, you might hear Rengarte reading the ceremony. Good afternoon, Briscoe."

Schwenk got up to go. He looked over the eight prisoners and chuckled. He turned and started through the doorway.

"Schwenk," cried Briscoe. "You can't do that to her."

"If her own father doesn't object, why should you? Goodbye, Briscoe. I'll be too busy to see you again."

The door slammed. A lock rattled.

Mike Goddard muttered, "Rengarte ain't no priest. Anybody can see he ain't. She won't be fooled by that."

"If he shaved," said Briscoe, "he'd fool anybody. Banjo! Can't you do something about these locks?"

"What have I been doing for a week?" complained Banjo. "Knitting?"

"If you could lift that stone there, Mike," said Briscoe, "you could bang it down on this chain—"

"We tried that and the stone's too soft," said Mike.

"Tim," pleaded Briscoe, "can't you work a bolt out of the wall?"

"That ain't coral," said Tim. "That's concrete. You might know that Swiney would think of all them things before we would. There ain't any way out of here at all, Briscoe. You been scurrying around like a squirrel in a cage looking for a way out and you can't expect a new one to jump up and crack you one. Besides, how would we get out of the cavern down there?"

"I'd swim for it!"

"You'd swim," said Mike, "about two feet, straight into the mouth of a shark. Now quiet down. Going nutty isn't going to get you anywhere."

"But I can't sit here and let Schwenk go ahead with that farce. Maybe I could tell that girl that Rengarte—"

"You couldn't tell her anything," said Banjo. "She wouldn't believe you if you said white was white."

"That's right," agreed Mike. "And besides, I'm not worried about any dame. I just want to get out, that's all."

"Banjo," said Briscoe, "what did you do with those keys when they caught you outside of the gun shed?"

"Threw 'em into the brush. Think I wanted them to find them on me?"

"And they're still there?"

"Unless Schwenk took a magnet to find them," said Banjo.

"Look here," said Briscoe. "You've got to help me. If all of us hauled in on these bolts of mine, maybe I could pull them—"

"Jesus," said Mike, "you're going crazy! We tried that the first night, don't you remember? Forget about that dame. You can't help her. We've got a whole week, maybe more, and Schwenk might let us go after—"

"Mike," said Tim Sullivan. "I've known you for five years at least and if I've said it once, I've said it five hundred times. Just bein' optimistic won't get you out of a hole. You've got to do something besides wish. You know just as well as I do that old Schwenk wouldn't let us live if he was to get ten thousand dollars cash apiece for us. I told you something like this would happen. We was doing all right. And you had to go and get this crazy idea and Briscoe had to get romantic and try to steal a skirt right out from under Swiney's nose and here we are. That's what comes of bein' hopeful, I tell you."

"Aw, we had a good chance," defended Mike.

"We did not!" disputed Tim.

"Then why'd you come in on it?" said Mike.

"Because . . . well . . . Anyhow, you won't bite these chains in two with your bare teeth."

Banjo sighed, "If I only had a file." He squared himself against the wall and brightened up. "They put me in jail once down in Rio. 'Dobe walls three feet thick, a window too small to squeeze through, a lock on the door that took a key as big as your arm. They sure had me that time. They was going to put me in front of a firing squad after the judge decided I really had killed the guy. It wasn't a very fair trial because they never let me talk at all. They just let a cop up and say that he'd seen the corpse with the knife in it, and they had a dance hall dame say that, yes, she seen me do it, and there I was.

"But I fooled them. They were going to use me for a target at dawn sharp, and while it was still dark they sent a priest in to me so I could confess. The priest was a funny little guy with a voice way down in his boots. He says, 'Son, to me you can confess your sins.' He give me a brass crucifix to hold and I knelt down and made up a lot of stuff and pretty soon, when I'd finished, he grumbles, 'My son, is there any last request I can fulfill?'

"Right then I saw light. I says, 'Yes, Father, there is one last request. Allow me to have a half-hour in which to pray and then let me die with this holy cross clutched agin my sinful breast.'

"So he says, 'My son, that is okay with me,' and he leaves me the cross and I knelt down until he got out of sight.

"It was still pretty dark and I began to pray in a loud voice so the guard outside couldn't hear what else I was doing. You know how flimsy they make their jail crucifixes in Rio. Well, it wasn't any trick at all to bend out one of the feet and one of the hands and stick that there cross right into the lock. I turned it and I was free just like that.

"I batted the guard over the head with it, took his rifle and lammed for the beach. I got aboard an outbound freighter just one gulp and a gasp ahead of the police.

"I never did think much of religion until then, but I know it's mighty useful now."

"But you ain't got any cross," growled Tim. "So why bring it up just to make us feel bad."

They were quiet after that. They could hear the waves mourning down in the cavern. Overhead, at times, they could hear footsteps.

Briscoe tried to sleep, but he had too much to think about. For hours he lay staring at the dark roof as though trying to project his thoughts through it.

As nearly as Briscoe could figure, it must have been early morning when the door creaked again.

First he saw a candle and then, behind and above it, a face. Diana!

The upcast golden light made a halo about her head. Her eyes were too bright and frightened.

She stopped, held the candlestick higher.

"Briscoe," she whispered.

With a harsh rattle and clank of chains, the eight sat up. Their hollowed eyes and sunken cheeks and unshaven faces made a terrifying picture against the rough wall.

Diana stepped back hurriedly, almost dropping the candle.

"It's all right," said Briscoe soothingly. "These irons have held for a week. They'll hold another five minutes."

"I saw Josef come down by that door last night," whispered Diana. "He said that you were dead. He said your longboat had been found overturned on the banks of the Zaga River. There are five searching parties of natives out looking for you."

Briscoe's heart began to beat faster. Eagerly he sat forward, straining at the iron which held him. "If you tell them where we are, they'll attack and free us!"

"I . . . I can't do that. They would murder Schwenk."

"Good!" spat Mike. "Don't hold off on my account."

"But I couldn't let them do that," said Diana. "Josef has been very kind . . . and . . . and after all, you mutinied and tried to murder all of us."

"Then you believe that," said Briscoe, harshly. "You believe Schwenk, the filthiest cutthroat in the Celebes. And I suppose tonight you'll marry him."

Diana stood straighter. "I came here to find if there was anything I could do to lessen your misery. I have worried about it since the night I saw the longboat put into the cavern below and then come out empty. But I did not come here to listen to you curse a man who has been of the greatest aid to both my father and me."

"You believe he'll really marry you?" snapped Briscoe.

"What do you mean?"

"You didn't know that Schwenk already has a wife in Australia?"

"How could you know that? You are trying to turn me against him so I will procure your release."

"Tonight," said Briscoe, "you will be 'married' by a former veterinarian in the French Army. A man named Rengarte."

"You cannot malign a priest!" said Diana.

"You came here this morning to help me," said Briscoe. "If you believed everything which has been said about me, you would not have given the matter another thought."

"I was . . . I think your punishment is just. A Dutch jail may teach you that loyalty is a better course."

"Not a Dutch jail," said Briscoe. "That's another lie. Schwenk is going to feed us to the sharks, no matter what he tells you about it. If you go through with this marriage, if you turn aside everything I say to you—"

"You cannot play upon my sympathies, Mr. Briscoe. I have seen too much about you and your companions in Josef's papers. Wanted men. Renegades. Thieves and murderers. Oh, I've seen the posted reward papers. Mike Goddard, Tim Sullivan, the notorious Banjo Edwards."

"But you've seen nothing about me," said Briscoe.

"You are mistaken. Josef has just received your complete record from Nordyke, captain of the *Rangoon*. I was mistaken about you. You do not merit aid, Mr. Briscoe. I hope . . . I hope the Dutch courts give you life!"

She tossed her head angrily, turned to the door and opened it. "To think that I came here to help a liar as well as a criminal. To think you would dare suggest that I aid you in starting a wholesale mutiny among the workmen. I am sorry that I troubled you, Mr. Briscoe."

Mike groaned when she had gone. "You said the wrong thing, Lee. You ain't got any tact at all. 'Course she thinks Schwenk's a damned saint. He wouldn't show her anything crude until he had her, would he? 'Course she thinks you're a liar. Good God, Briscoe, you ain't no diplomat at all. Why didn't you moan and whimper and say you was sorry you'd been bad and that Schwenk was a good, kind man and you only wanted a chance . . . ?"

Clink!
Clank!
Rattle!

"There," said Banjo, with a sigh of relief.

They whirled and stared at him and saw that the impossible had happened. Banjo's irons were in a heap about him and Banjo was free!

"How the devil . . . ?" began Briscoe.

Banjo moved stiffly across the chamber and knelt at Briscoe's side, tugging at the bracelets.

"What happened?" demanded Briscoe. "Have you been holding out on us?"

"Me?" said Banjo, grieved. "Women are saints. I never thought they was much use, but now I'm a changed man. I'll go through life hand in hand with women and religion, s'help me. You made her mad. She tossed her head, zip, like that and . . ."

Grinning, Banjo held up a hairpin.

"They shed 'em like a dog sheds hair," grinned Banjo, slipping the unlocked irons from Briscoe's wrists.

CHAPTER SIX

To the Chatter of Machine Guns

WHEN Banjo had successfully picked the lock of every man's irons, Briscoe signaled for silence.

The natives were hard to suppress. They grinned and capered and chuckled, but they finally understood that this was but the first step to their freedom.

Briscoe rubbed his chafed wrists and ankles, trying to exercise some of the stiffness from his body. Then, again motioning for silence, he moved toward the tunnel which led into the caverns below.

Quietly he made his way around the first bend. He knelt and peered around the second. He drew back hastily and crept to the top.

"There's a Kanaka guard down there on the landing," he whispered to Mike. "He's got a machine gun pointed straight up the incline."

"We'll rush him," said Mike.

"And run for a hundred feet in plain view of him?" said Briscoe. "It won't work."

Banjo grinned and waved the twisted hairpin. He slid to the door leading upward, thrust the metal into the big lock and then dejectedly shook his head.

"There's a key turned in the other side," said Banjo.

"And even if we made it," muttered Tim, "Schwenk would be standing there waiting for us."

"Can't you think of something?" pleaded Briscoe.

Banjo stood up, shut his eyes tightly and pulled his nose. Mike scratched impatiently. Tim sat down and held his head in his hands. The natives expectantly watched Briscoe and Briscoe watched Banjo.

They were an unholy-looking crew in the greenish light which came up from the cavern below. Gaunt, red-eyed and ragged, one glimpse of them would have made a stone idol quake.

Banjo snapped his fingers, then shook his head, rejecting his thought. He looked brightly up again.

Banjo got down on his knees and sniffed along the bottom of the door. Quickly, he peeled off his shirt and thrust it through the wide crack so that it made a carpet on the other side.

Banjo reached into the keyhole with his hairpin and worked deftly at the key.

It dropped out and fell with a small, dull sound on Banjo's shirt. Working with great care, he retrieved his garment and there solidly upon it was the large key.

Admiration made even Tim Sullivan smile.

Instantly, however, as an apology for it, Tim said, "You mark my words. Schwenk will be waiting for us on the other side."

Banjo unlocked the door and shoved it open.

A blast of daylight blinded them. Hurriedly they stepped back out of the way of probable bullets. But when they could see well in the light, they were astounded to discover that the hall before them was quite empty.

Working with great care, he retrieved his garment and there solidly upon it was the large key.

Briscoe took the lead. As soundless as a stalking cat he crept along the hardwood planks, stopping every few feet to listen. He came to another door and tried it.

The dismal rattle of a chain came from the other side. Briscoe stepped back in despair. Not even the nimble-fingered expert could unfasten this barrier.

Banjo looked sadly at the lock. Tried it. Turning to Tim, Banjo said, "Looks like we'll never find out if you're right about Swiney being on the other side."

"Look," said Briscoe. "It swings out. If three of us lunge against it at the same time, something's bound to let loose."

"Our shoulders at least," said Mike.

In spite of the noise it would make, risking everything for their freedom, Briscoe, Tim and Mike drew back. Briscoe counted, "One . . . two . . . three!"

Bam!

The door caved. In a tangle of arms and legs they lit on top of it, breath knocked completely out.

Briscoe tried to struggle up. Certainly the racket would bring somebody to investigate. He got to his feet and braced himself for an attack.

But the house remained silent.

Puzzled by the lack of a reception, the eight went cautiously ahead to find themselves in the cellar of the house.

"He'll be waiting at the top of the stairs," said Tim.

"I'll see," said Briscoe, ascending.

Another door was there, but it was half open. Through it Briscoe could see a gleaming expanse of floor, some scattered furniture and rugs, but no sign whatever of Schwenk.

"Come up," said Briscoe to the others.

Irresolutely they gathered in the living room. Then, like zombies, they drifted several ways through the house.

Banjo came back eating an immense sandwich and swigging at a bottle of red wine. Tim returned dragging the yellow servant, Wong.

The slant-eyed little Oriental was terrified. He could not talk. He could only gasp and blink and gulp. He fell to his knees and raised his hands. His mouth open and shut like a goldfish's.

"Where is Schwenk?" demanded Briscoe.

"M-m-m . . . gug!" said Wong, shaking like a flivver's fender.

"Nuts," said Briscoe in disgust. He picked up a pair of field glasses from a side table and went up a second flight of stairs to Schwenk's lookout.

The island appeared completely deserted. No natives could be seen around the slave huts. Not a single white was on the beach. There were two ships in the harbor. One was the *Sultan*, the other was Schwenk's *Rangoon*. Smoke poured out of the *Sultan*'s spindly funnel, but she was still fast to the dock.

Briscoe trained the glasses on the northernmost point of land. He lowered them quickly.

Schwenk was coming along the beach. Diana and Martin were with him. Behind the three mounted people came a long column of natives carrying a dark, oblong box.

"What the devil!" said Briscoe.

Behind him, Mike took a look.

"It's a coffin," said Mike.

"But who's dead?" said Briscoe.

Tim had come up the stairs. Mournfully, Tim said, "You are."

"Who?" snapped Briscoe.

"You," sighed Tim.

Briscoe ran down the stairs and met Banjo. The moon-faced little man was laughing uproariously. He had Wong by the collar.

"Tell . . . tell him," choked Banjo, between blasting guffaws.

"Briscoe dead," quivered Wong. "Native boy findum Briscoe on Zaga all ate up by ants."

"Tell him!" choked Banjo.

"D-D-Dead man—"

"Tell him who it is!"

Wong shriveled up and whined, "Master killum doc. Doc fellah askum hushee-hushee money. Me and master killum, dragum along Zaga las' night."

"He killed Rengarte!" shouted the hysterical Banjo.

Mike and Tim were coming down fast.

"What's happened?" demanded Mike.

Briscoe jerked his thumb at Wong. "He says he and Schwenk murdered Rengarte. Schwenk needed a body to fix up like me. He had to convince the natives I was dead from causes he had nothing to do with. He let ants eat the corpse and now they're bringing the corpse back. Rengarte tried to blackmail him."

"We'll get the guns and when Schwenk comes up, we'll shoot him," said Mike. "It's easy."

"Nothing of the kind," said Briscoe. "Under no conditions shoot Schwenk. Keep him alive."

"What the hell?" argued Mike. "We got to act quick.

They'll be up here in ten minutes. Schwenk's got the crews of the *Sultan* and *Rangoon* for protection. Those Kanakas are armed and they'll fight. They've got us outnumbered. We'll have to shoot Schwenk—"

"I'll kill the first man," said Briscoe, "who tries to kill Schwenk. Is that understood?"

"Jesus, I didn't know you was that serious about it," gulped Mike. "What kind of a dizzy setup is this? First he couldn't kill you, but now that he can, you won't kill him. Is it that dame?"

"No," said Briscoe. "It isn't that dame. Look alive, Banjo. Find those keys you threw away. We're going to take the *Sultan*."

Banjo scurried outside and dived into a tangle of brush. He came up with the tailored keys, unlocked the gun shed and quickly picked the rack padlocks which held the rifles and pistols. All automatics were gone, evidently in the possession of the loyal Kanakas.

They had very little time to get to the dock. Already, Schwenk was close enough to see them plainly if they went into the open.

Buckling on a bandolier of ammunition and carrying an Enfield, Briscoe led the way toward the *Sultan*, the other seven running swiftly after him.

They swept down the curving roadway and into Schwenk's sight.

Briscoe heard the far-off bellow of orders. He saw three men detach themselves from the column and throw themselves into the sand.

An instant later came the rattling explosions of automatic rifles.

Bullets ripped through the palms and plowed sand. Water frothed over the dock. Air crackled overhead.

"Come on!" yelled Briscoe, boots hammering on the planks.

Over the *Sultan*'s rail glittered a gun barrel. Behind the sight glinted the off-color eye of Captain Gunarson.

"I've got you!" roared Gunarson in triumph.

Briscoe dodged, but the machine-gun barrel whipped down, following him. Gunarson squeezed the trigger.

Less than a dozen shots left the muzzle.

One shot rapped sharply from the dock.

Banjo yelled a derisive "The hell you have!"

Gunarson's collapsed face slid out of sight under the rail.

Screened from Schwenk by the ship, the eight sprinted up the gangplank, yelling, holding their rifles on high.

A Kanaka rose up as though ready to give battle. He took one look at the eight demons and threw down his rifle in surrender.

Tim raced up the bridge ladder and ducked into the pilothouse. Mike plunged down through a hatch toward the engine room. Two shots sounded below decks. Mike yelled, "Got him!"

Banjo grabbed up a fire ax and hacked through the bow hawser. Briscoe scooped the dead Gunarson's weapon out of the scupper, raised the sights to shoot high and drove the Kanakas from the beach with scorching lead.

Banjo had the stern hawsers away. A bell jangled. Mike in the engine room jangled back.

The *Sultan* drew out into the stream.

Briscoe stopped firing and looked around. Two Kanakas had very quietly come out of the fo'c's'le and were now engaged in coiling up what was left of the hemp. The Kanaka who had surrendered, also a diplomat, had reported for duty to Tim as quartermaster.

Out of the engine room hatch crept a half-breed engineer who had been left in charge by Gunarson. He had two bullets through the fleshy part of his arm and he docilely asked for treatment, giving no sign whatever of his late objection to Mike.

Briscoe eyed the shore and saw that two longboats were putting out for the anchored *Rangoon*. Schwenk had not given up by any means.

Briscoe looked at his crew. The four natives were wrist-deep in a ten pound can of corned beef and a box of sea biscuits, but their rifles were near at hand and, from time to time, they glanced at Briscoe as though anxious to follow any order he had to give.

"They're following us," said Banjo, looking at the swinging shore, and then at the *Rangoon*.

From the pilothouse, Tim leaned out and yelled, "There comes the *Rangoon*, Briscoe. Gunwales awash with Kanakas! We'll play the devil getting away from those guys."

Mike stepped out of the hatch like Punch. "She's doing all she can."

"Tie down the safety valves!" ordered Briscoe.

"Okay," said Mike. "If you're willing to go to hell by the high-line route, I'm right with you." He disappeared.

CHAPTER SEVEN

Desperate Bid for Escape

A bone boiled in the *Rangoon*'s plowing teeth. With steam already up, she had been able to slip her cable and swing seaward in a matter of minutes.

Less than a thousand yards behind the laboring *Sultan*, Schwenk was taking advantage of the short range. Nervous splatters of machine-gun bullets sent the paint chips soaring from the plates and superstructure of the fleeing steamer.

"We can't make it!" wailed Tim.

"Hey, the boat's crew!" shouted Briscoe to the natives. "Swing out that gig and turn over her engine in the davits."

The natives jumped toward the small boat which was cradled on the upper deck.

Briscoe turned about and ran aft. He planted the machine gun on the fantail and crouched behind it in the protection of jumbled hawsers.

With quick, raking bursts he splintered every glass in the *Rangoon*'s pilothouse. The answering fire from the *Rangoon*'s chain lockers spattered brightly into steel, thumped angrily into the hemp.

Banjo squirmed aft on his stomach. His voice was strained and the words he said were punctuated by crackling slugs.

"There's a Dutch gunboat two cable lengths away, two

points off our bows. She's blocking the channel. I saw her crew stripping a three-inch gun!"

Briscoe poured another burst into the *Rangoon* and then snaked backward, Banjo helping him to drag the machine gun.

They scrambled up a ladder to the bridge. Briscoe glared stormily at the sleek hull which waited like a starved shark for them.

"I knew it," moaned Tim. "Schwenk behind us, a gunboat ahead of us. We can't swim for it. They'll board us and murder us to a man."

"They sure will," agreed Banjo.

Mike came up, mopping black grease from his hairy hands. He saw the gunboat and stopped dead.

"Jesus! What luck we do have. There hasn't been a gunboat in these waters for almost a year and this one shows up right on the dot. You'd think it was sent for!"

"It was," said Briscoe. "Come on, there's no time to stand around yammering about it. Into that gig."

"Gig?" gaped Tim. "You mean you'll go to sea in a gig?"

"We're going ashore," stated Briscoe, slapping the machine gun down in the small boat's bow. "Engine all right?"

The stroke oar of the black longboat crew nodded jerkily. His three mates were riveting their bulging eyes upon the gunboat's sleek hull.

"Ashore?" gaped Tim. "You mean we're going ashore? You mean you'll put Schwenk on our trail direct?"

Briscoe motioned toward the beach. It was about a thousand yards away. The water which flanked the channel swirled ominously in spots, marking hidden fragments of reef. The surf was breaking directly on the sand. Behind that an impenetrable wall of heat-distorted jungle spread its thick tangle over the mountains like a blanket.

"Half speed," said Briscoe. "Hard astarboard. Head straight in toward the beach. With this ship protecting us from the gunboat's shells, we've got a chance to make it."

"But the *Rangoon*'s guns!" cried Tim.

"Damn the *Rangoon*'s guns!" barked Briscoe. "Half speed! Hard astarboard! Lower away!"

The *Sultan* swung at right angles to her course and plowed through the reef-fanged water toward the sand.

The gunboat let drive. A three-inch shell moaned overhead and exploded before the bows.

The whites, the black men and the brown Kanakas swarmed into the gig. They lowered away. The racing water clutched their keel and tore them from the blocks. The boat's engine raced, grabbed water and thrust ahead.

A second shell whined on its way. It struck the *Sultan*'s pilothouse. Glass, splinters, chips of lead and steel ripped the air. The superstructure collapsed. Tardily came the gun's boom.

Still screened by the destruction-bent steamer from the gunboat, the gig, steering through jagged coral outcrops, sped for shore.

The *Rangoon*'s gunners suddenly understood. The water about the gig began to spatter as though beaten by rain. The gunwale caved in. The sea swiftly roared through the breach.

Briscoe grabbed the tiller. He had to get the boat ashore before it filled completely.

The *Sultan* hit a section of the reef, plowed into it, fell off on its side. A third shell made mincemeat out of the fantail.

Unable to follow through the shallow water, the *Rangoon* pulled up and put its gig over.

Briscoe shouted for his men to bail.

It appeared to be impossible to make the shore. Still fifty yards out, still in deep, turbulent water, the gig was foundering.

The gunboat had caught sight of the exposed gig, and its fourth shot geysered not ten feet away, almost sinking the ship's boat.

A mighty, towering wave dipped under the gig's stern and lifted it high.

With a roaring rush, with the foam breaking on their heads, the men were catapulted, boat and all, straight at the sand. They hit at about thirty miles an hour, knocking the gig to splinters, pitching them out on dry land.

They grabbed their rifles and the machine gun. Sand spurted under their feet as the *Rangoon*'s gig began to fire.

Briscoe reached the jungle and swept his men into cover behind him. He dug down the tripod legs of the machine gun, gripped the butts, squeezed hard on the trigger.

Water foamed all about the *Rangoon*'s gig. Hastily it about-faced and raced back.

The gunboat slid through the water toward the *Rangoon*. It looked as though the two ships put their heads together to think up a new way of seizing the mutineers.

Briscoe withdrew into the brush. Banjo had found a thickly overgrown trail, but not one man made a move to go down it.

"Where to?" said Mike.

"If Schwenk finds out exactly where we are and how many there are of us and what guns we've got," said Tim, "he'll be after us like a bloodhound."

"He'll know very shortly," said Briscoe.

"How so?" demanded Mike.

"Because," said Briscoe, inspecting the machine-gun belt, "the Kanakas are gone."

"Why, the dirty—" began Mike.

"Let them go," said Briscoe. "Gentlemen, we're not licked yet."

CHAPTER EIGHT

Briscoe Goes Alone

"I guess," said Mike, solemnly scratching under his arm, "that this just about washes up the works. Me, I'm a diehard, but when it comes to running up against Schwenk, the armed Kanakas of two steamers, twenty armed white men *and* the officers and crew of a Dutch gunboat, I just can't seem to work up any enthusiasm about our prospects."

"I knew we'd all get killed sooner or later," said Tim, morosely, "but I didn't know the execution was goin' to be so damned emphatic."

Banjo had nothing at all to say about it. For the first time the other three whites and the native boat's crew noticed that Banjo was carrying a weighty sack and seemed to have disposed of his Enfield and bandolier.

Banjo set down the sack in a clearing. It was a canvas sea bag, some four feet long, and it bulged unto bursting. Round, pasty face perfectly sober, Banjo began to extract things. He had a big roll of bills he had taken from the well-locked ship's safe. He had a Very pistol and a box of shells. He had a pearl scarf pin.

Banjo rolled up his sleeves and dived again into the bag. He began to produce rapidly now. He stacked up a pile which consisted of dried beef, sea biscuits, strawberry jam, four shirts, four pairs of white pants, two razors, shaving soap, a mother-of-pearl knife, a belaying pin, three rings of keys, ten sticks of dynamite with caps and fuses terrifyingly attached, numerous papers, a sack of pearls, a gold watch, a silver pitcher, a dispatch box, a set of brass knuckles, a file, a can of sardines, a compass, two pairs of tennis shoes, a magazine, a pair of field glasses, two pairs of socks, a seaman's cap, a ball of twine and a flashlight.

Banjo paused and sighed, "Doggone it, they must be in here someplace."

He dived again and came up triumphantly holding a sheaf of papers.

"What's that?" demanded Briscoe.

"They was on Swiney's desk. Copies of radiograms he sent out on the *Rangoon*'s wireless." Banjo handed them over, adding, "I thought we might want to know where we stood."

Briscoe scanned them. His mouth went tight and his eyes blazed. "Damn him. *That's* why that gunboat was out in the channel!"

"Why?" said Mike.

"When Rengarte acted up, Schwenk killed him and radioed to Borneo asking that a gunboat come in to help him quiet matters down."

"Is that all?" said Tim.

"No. He asked the gunboat to bring him a minister."

"That's that dame's hard luck," said Mike. "Don't you go getting any romantic ideas. We're in enough trouble as it is. If she's sap enough to love old Swiney, it's just too bad."

"She doesn't love him," snapped Briscoe. "She's marrying

him because she thinks she's helping out her foster father. Martin is going to get fifty thousand dollars from Schwenk."

"That's a lot of bucks for a dame," said Mike. "But it ain't none of your business, Briscoe. We maybe can swipe a small boat and lam for British North Borneo across the strait. I'm for that. You're a good guy, Briscoe, but if you think you're a knight-errant on a galumphing horse, ready to jump into a dragon's mouth to rescue a fair damsel, it's quits."

"You won't go through with it?" demanded Briscoe.

"No," said Tim.

"I . . . I guess not," said Banjo.

"Okay," said Briscoe. "Okay. You're right. If you can steal a sailing canoe along the coast tonight, you may be able to make Tawan before dawn and be in British territory. God help you if you miss it."

"What?" gulped Mike. "Ain't you coming along?"

"No," said Briscoe.

"But Schwenk will shoot you on sight!" yelped Tim.

"That gunboat captain will string you up for piracy!" cried Banjo.

"No dame's worth it," said Mike.

"If I think different, that's my hard luck," said Briscoe.

Without further parley, Briscoe helped himself to a razor, shirt, pants, socks and tennis shoes. He went down to a nearby jungle stream and cleaned himself up.

The others watched him sadly. When he had changed himself into something which looked more like a gentleman, Briscoe tossed back the razor, picked up an Enfield, inspected the chamber, buckled on a bandolier, lashed an automatic to his thigh, and gave them a pale, gaunt grin.

"I hope you make it," said Briscoe. Abruptly he turned and strode up the winding, overgrown trail.

The four natives looked helpless and deserted. Banjo, Mike and Tim avoided each other's eyes. Briscoe's footsteps faded out.

CHAPTER NINE

While Torches Flare

PERHAPS if the gunboat had not been there, Briscoe would have gathered up the five hundred natives and led them in an attack against the big stone house.

But five hundred natives armed with knives would have little show against the small army of well-armed men with which Schwenk had suddenly surrounded himself.

On the path from the beach, shifting shadows in the dark, two Dutch sailors and two Kanakas were alertly on guard.

Behind the house a machine gun was planted for action. From a dark upstairs window protruded a rifle barrel. Higher up in the lookout the silhouette of another machine gunner could be seen.

It was a strange setting for a wedding, thought Briscoe, slipping quietly through the bushes which lined the curving road. A martial marriage, indeed, with an arch of guns instead of the bower of swords.

One man had about as much chance of breaking up the affair as he would have swimming the length of the shark-ripped lagoon. But Briscoe did not seem to realize that.

He reached the porch without being seen and crouched in the spot where he had first learned of Martin's identity and intentions. It was not a very safe spot. Through the thin leaves, he could see the shoes of the Dutch sailor who did guard duty there.

From time to time he could hear Schwenk's laugh within the house, accompanied by the lesser laughter of the gunboat's officers and Martin.

That irritated Briscoe. Schwenk was not at all worried about picking up the mutineers. Schwenk felt so secure and powerful that he could wait for another day, another week. Schwenk knew that starvation would show them up sooner or later. He had already learned where they were and it was only a matter of trailing.

Right now, Schwenk was much more interested in bringing off this marriage successfully while the gunboat was still in port. Flattered by the prospect of possessing such a beautiful bride, Schwenk expanded and let the wine flow, let fall who may.

Footsteps sounded almost at Briscoe's head. He glanced up and hurriedly drew back. Diana was in plain sight at the rail. But she was in light and he was in shadow and he passed unnoticed.

"I don't believe it," said Diana.

"But you saw his body, didn't you?" said Martin.

"That could not have been Briscoe. I . . . I saw Briscoe. . . . I mean, he was one of those men who got away."

"Nonsense. And besides, my dear, those men were all caught and shot. There is not the least bit of danger."

"I am not worried about the danger. It . . . it chills me, this place. So brutal and harsh, nothing soft about it. I . . . I can't go through with it."

Briscoe's heart lurched heavily and beat hopefully.

"My dear," purred Martin, "I am only too glad to do as you wish. Anything for your happiness. That is all that means anything to me. I shall go back to Sydney and give myself up. What is that, compared to your pleasure?"

"Oh, no," Diana gasped. "I can't let you do that."

"Schwenk will give you everything you want," said Martin. "I was thinking of that. I can give you nothing but my fatherly care. But if for one moment you have a doubt about the wisdom of this affair, I shall tell Schwenk about it immediately and we shall leave for Sydney tomorrow on the *Rangoon*."

"No. I'm being selfish, that is all. Forgive me. See, they are all waiting inside. Let's go in."

"Only if it is your express wish," purred Martin.

"It . . . it is my wish," said Diana.

Briscoe looked through the leaves at the sentry's shoes. When they had passed him by, he slipped out, quickly rounded the end of the porch and gripped the rail over his head.

A wicker chaise longue was on his end of the veranda. He slid into the shadow behind it. By opening the wickerwork a little he could see into the open window. Beneath him paced the restless sentry, rifle glinting each time he stepped through the light.

"All ready?" cried Schwenk, teetering a little, his bloated face flushed with alcohol. "Ah, then, let's get on with it."

Diana suffered him to take her arm. His cold, killer eyes flashed as he raked them over her, his lipless mouth twisted into a greedy grin.

Briscoe watched Diana. In his lifetime he had seen many, many girls, but none had affected him with more than a passing admiration. From the first time he had seen her on the deck of the *Sultan* until now, Briscoe had known that, whether she loved him or not, nothing would ever quite be the same again.

His hand was clenched on the sweaty butt of the .45 automatic. It would be so easy to shoot Schwenk, so pleasant to watch him die.

But a shot would measure his life in seconds. A crisscross fire would instantly follow from all sides of the house. He would be dead almost before he could release the trigger.

But even death was sometimes worth the price. But she would never know. Somehow, before he took that course, he would have to make her understand.

The minister the gunboat had brought was tall and scrawny and obviously of great piety. He opened his book, peered over his glasses and motioned for Schwenk and Diana to stand squarely before him. The white-suited officers formed a ring behind the couple, smiling, quiet now, but still with an eye on Schwenk's buffet.

The minister began. Briscoe drew his .45 and hefted it nervously.

The room was lighted by two tall candelabra which stood upon the buffet. Briscoe closed his mouth like a steel trap. He had made up his mind.

Shifting sideways behind the chaise longue, he took aim. The two thunderous explosions jarred almost together. Their bases struck, the candelabra toppled into sudden darkness.

Like a broken-field runner, Briscoe launched himself through the window and across the floor. Men went down like tenpins before him.

Even in the blackness it was not hard to find Diana. He swung her struggling body into his arms, whirled and raced toward the door.

Had it remained dark, he might have succeeded.

As it was, three flashlights pinned him in the doorway from the outside.

Desperately, he whirled and tried to go back through the room. Two sentries plunged into his path from the rear of the house, their torch beams playing over him.

A fixed bayonet prodded him in the back. The candles were lighted.

"Oho!" said Schwenk. "Hello, Briscoe. Just in time, Briscoe. Have a drink? This is Briscoe, gentlemen. A playful chap, this Briscoe. You know, the murderer I was telling you about. But very playful. Have a drink, Briscoe, because, as soon as you put my wife down, I think I'll kill you."

Diana was crying into Briscoe's shoulder. All the nervous strength she had had was exhausted.

Brokenly, she said, "They . . . they tried to make me believe . . . Oh, I've been a fool. . . . You . . . did this for me! You can't be what they say you are. You can't! I've dreamed that someday I'd find out they were lying. I do not believe them now. Whatever they do to you, Briscoe, I'll be with you."

They pried her away from him. The Dutch captain, von Kroll, stood importantly in front of Briscoe and looked him up and down.

*Two sentries plunged into his path from the rear
of the house, their torch beams playing over him.
A fixed bayonet prodded him in the back.*

"Murderer, eh? Deserted from the Army, eh? We've remedies for that. You've shot men. You've tried piracy. But I'll show you what they do to pirates and murderers."

Schwenk was fingering Briscoe's automatic.

The machine gunner who had been upstairs came down. The sentries were all in from the walk. They made a hollow square around Briscoe, bayonets menacing him.

"Captain," said Briscoe. "You've got to listen to me. I am First Lieutenant Fremont of the United States Army."

"I know," said von Kroll, with a satisfied smirk. "And you deserted. I have authority to deal with criminals—"

"I am not a deserter," said Briscoe, steadily. "I am on a year's leave of absence. Warren Fremont was my father."

"Ho, but I have you there," said von Kroll. "The man died of fever."

"That's right," said Schwenk, carelessly noting if a shell was in the automatic chamber and wondering just how he could make Briscoe run for it.

"He did not die of fever," said Briscoe. "Warren Fremont was murdered by an ex-officer in the Prussian Army named Schwenk."

"I'm afraid you can't prove that," said von Kroll.

"Very funny, isn't he?" said Schwenk. "Very witty, Briscoe. Very witty."

"In San Francisco," said Briscoe, "Warren Fremont left a note in a safe-deposit box which stated that he was afraid of this new overseer Schwenk and that Schwenk should be investigated in event of my father's death. That was a long time ago. I also thought my father had died from fever. That was five years ago. I finally saved money enough for the trip and managed to procure a year's leave to investigate this island."

"Hah, but you're lying there," said von Kroll. "You should have come to the Dutch courts, you see."

"The Dutch courts have no authority over this island," snapped Briscoe.

"What?" roared von Kroll.

"Timba is a part of the Sulu Archipelago," stated Briscoe. "It was expressly deeded to the United States by Spain in 1899 as part of the Philippine Islands. It was purchased outright by my grandfather at that time as a copra plantation. Since then it has been lost to all but nautical charts. Because it is close to Borneo, Schwenk made the error of thinking it must belong to the Dutch. He murdered my father, imported slaves from Africa—"

"Bah," snorted von Kroll. "You have nothing to prove this."

"Not a thing," said Schwenk with a twisted grin.

"I had those papers in my baggage. Every one of them. But Schwenk searched and evidently found them and destroyed them."

"Get on with this, will you, Captain?" said Schwenk. "The fool stole a ship, you know, shot my men . . ."

"Of course. Guard, remove this man to the ship. We will hold court in the morning and dispense with the trouble of taking him to Borneo." von Kroll turned around.

Everyone had been facing Briscoe. Von Kroll's face went white as paper. His jaw dropped. A glass fell from his fingers and shattered on the floor.

• THE BOLD DARE ALL •

Outside a growing mutter could be heard. Nervously, the guard remembered that not one man had been left outside.

Slowly, everyone followed von Kroll's horror-bulged eyes.

Sitting at the head of the steps, on the tripod of a machine gun, was Mike.

Juggling a stick of dynamite, Tim was perched upon a windowsill.

Carrying his immense sea bag, Banjo pushed through the crowd from the back door.

Torches were blazing on the drive. Torches flared and smoked on every side of the house. Five hundred natives swung their shining knives and strained their necks to make sure that Briscoe was really alive. They saw him. Their yells rolled like thunder. But they kept back until they received orders.

Mike scratched his stomach and suggestively swiveled the blue snout of the weapon. Tim leaned against the sill and hopelessly looked at the officers and men.

Von Kroll found his voice. "Damn you! My gunboat—"

"Ain't been in operation for more than ten minutes," said Banjo, setting down his bag.

Diana, finding herself free, stepped to Briscoe's side and smiled triumphantly at the crowd.

"Briscoe," said Banjo. "Maybe these is the papers you was looking for."

He reached into the sea bag and hauled out a pile of odds and ends, wallets, watches and other things he had picked up while passing through the crowd.

He handed over a leather case on which the initials L. B. F. were stamped.

Briscoe whooped for joy. He snatched out a map, a deed, letters, old reports and treaty copies and thrust them under von Kroll's quivering nose.

Von Kroll sniffed at them, rather than looked them over. But he found them to be right and correct and indisputable and he began to be very worried about his gunboat down there in American waters.

Until that moment, everyone had forgotten Schwenk. But Schwenk saw his fate written in von Kroll's hands. He whipped up the automatic and, in spite of the machine gun, backed toward the door.

"Damn you!" screamed Schwenk. "Damn you, Briscoe! You can't touch me. You can't. I said I'd kill you and I will!"

Mike could not fire without killing others.

Not a man moved.

Schwenk's finger was coming down on the trigger and Briscoe was squarely in his sights.

It happened in split seconds.

A black arm snaked into the doorway. The grinning, gloating black face of the giant Joffo darted up over Schwenk's shoulder.

The hand struck at the instant Schwenk fired. The bullet furrowed the ceiling.

As though vanished in thin air, Schwenk disappeared.

They could hear him scream as he was dragged down the path. They were blasted by the roar which greeted Schwenk from five hundred throats.

Shadows swarmed on the curving road. Torches smoked and flamed. Knives flashed.

Mike grinned. "Captain," he said, "you can get that gunboat of yours the hell out of here any time you want to. We got matters under control now. These Kanakas won't make any fight, and Briscoe . . ."

Von Kroll looked quickly at Briscoe and Diana and then started to leave.

"Hell," said Tim. "You always were dumb, Mike. They can't take that minister away. Briscoe needs him."

The minister, thoroughly frightened, looked about for his book.

Sheepishly, Banjo pulled it out of the sea bag and handed it across.

Story Preview

NOW that you've just ventured through one of the captivating tales in the Stories from the Golden Age collection by L. Ron Hubbard, turn the page and enjoy a preview of *Fifty-Fifty O'Brien*. Join Winchester Remington Smith whose enemies are as predictable as ducks at a carnival shooting gallery. But he's neither prepared nor equipped to handle the likes of First Sergeant Fifty-Fifty O'Brien.

Fifty-Fifty O'Brien

THE coaster dip roared like HE shells in a barrage. The merry-go-round wheezed and banged soulfully and the cymbals clanged and the horns blazed away and the horses went up and down and the kids shouted.

The freak show barker delivered his hoarsely nasal spiel, never varying, never ending. The popcorn seller bawled his wares and the peanut roaster squealed with a shrill monotony which went through your head like a knife.

People shouted, people laughed. The hum of the midway went on and on, its pulsation an electric shock which made you breathe hard with excitement. The roulette wheels whirred and the trained seal barked.

And above it and through it went the *yap, yap, yap* of .22 rifles, hammering away with gusto at the mechanical ducks which swam and dived, and dived and swam, on their endless chain. Water geysered, bells clanged, lead whacked through clothespins, splinters sang.

And behind the cartridge-covered counter, on the muzzle side of the chained rifles, stood a young man with straw-colored hair and eyes that flared like gaslights. He was yelling to be heard above the racket, above the clang, above the showering tinkle of empties. He was hazy in the smoke and dust, but his voice was sharp and clear.

"C'mon, step right up and winnah a ceegah. Winnah a ceegah. Winnah baybee dawl. Two bits for fifteen shots. Heresya your chance. Heresyachance. Anybodeee can do it. Right this way, step right up."

Over and over. *Crack, crack, crack. Clang clang.* And the ducks and rabbits jumped up and went down, over and over again.

From the next booth, the grifter leaned out and yelled, "Hey, Win! Hear ya leavin' us."

"Yeah. Gonna join the Marines."

"Whatsa matter? Doncha like it?"

"Wanta see some excitement for a change, thasall."

Crack, crack, crack, the pungent smell of smokeless powder and dust and the buzz and clang and clatter of the crowd, the merry-go-round, the coaster dip, the people, the radios, the people, and *crack, crack, crack . . .*

Silence.

Nothing moved.

Brooding, festering jungle steamed unheard as it had for centuries. Vast, empty silence like a wall which roared and roared and hurt your ears. Tense, festering jungle—nothing else.

For a long while Winchester Remington Smith had been standing at the top of the trail, staring down through the twilight tunnel which was the trail. His sodden khaki, mud-spattered and torn, blended in with the tan and red of the muck in the path. His campaigner was faded, wavy from rain and sun, and his leggings were the color of Nicaragua.

• FIFTY-FIFTY O'BRIEN •

Somewhere ahead he had heard a sound. Ten minutes ago he had heard it. And he stood there, waiting, ears smarting with silence. In his hat he carried a few sheets of onionskin paper—orders for Company K. And the paper had to get through.

To push back that still wall which pressed in against him, he muttered, "The only difference between me and a telephone wire is that they patch a wire and bury a runner."

Bitterness marred his voice. For three months he had been at it—carrying orders, stamping alone across mountains, through angry yellow streams, down steep-sided, silent ravines.

And he was under orders to avoid trouble, to get his messages through.

But God, what a relief it would have been to send Springfield lead into a goonie's guts. Sometimes, when he crept alone through the sullen night, he almost went mad with the desire to fire a clip at the silence. Anything to break the tension before the tension broke him.

Perhaps, this time, when he got back to Company K, the top kick would let him stay around long enough to get himself back again. But Company K hardly knew him, and neither did "Fifty-Fifty" O'Brien, first sergeant USMC. And if Fifty-Fifty O'Brien didn't even see him, then what chance did a fellow have in getting a break?

Fifty-Fifty O'Brien. He'd like to know that man. Fifty-Fifty O'Brien was solid. He didn't let a thing like silence get him. Fifty-Fifty O'Brien was the toughest man in the regiment. Self-reliant, big-jawed, swashbuckling, with a killer's eyes—pale, icy eyes that stared straight through you and out the other side and saw something you couldn't see.

Fifty-Fifty O'Brien and his small black horse—the only black pony in the regiment—were always found in unexpected places. O'Brien had the idea that he himself could bring this guerrilla war to an end.

A faraway click of a hoof, faint in all this stillness, came again to Win Smith's ears. He moved the rifle a fraction of an inch, glanced down to make certain that the safety was off.

His pale, haggard eyes bored down through the leafy tunnel, and he crouched a little forward, waiting for he knew not what. The fact that something besides himself was moving in this vastness heartened him, made him forget the silence for a moment. Something was moving in the steamy heat and silence and it might spell danger.

He could hear the hoofs more distinctly, he could even see a shadow moving through the patterns of sun upon the path. Then he wanted to shout with relief. A black pony was coming toward him—and a black pony meant O'Brien. Maybe he'd have company during the last ten miles.

He started to call out a greeting, but the word clung in his throat, a sodden lump. O'Brien was not on the horse. The rider wore a straw hat, a ragged white shirt, a pair of leather puttees.

A goonie! On the black horse!

Where was O'Brien?

A creak of leather and a startled wheeze from the pony, a swift white flash of amazed eyes, the blur of a hand moving to the boot for a mountain gun.

Win Smith dropped down and the shot screamed over his head. The rifle jolted his shoulder, shaking the jungle with its crash.

The native jerked in the saddle, clawed at the horn, and came sliding out. The black horse, nostrils flared, charged up the trail toward Win Smith. He snatched at the bridle, caught it, and dragged the pony to a snorting stop.

Very slowly, very watchfully, he went down the red clay path toward the sprawled lump of white. For an instant he was afraid he had missed and killed the native, but the pale flicker of an eyelid gave him assurance. He knelt down and propped the goonie up against a tree trunk.

"What's the idea?" said Win Smith. "*¿Que pasó?*"

"*¡Yanqui!*" spat the goonie in a spray of blood.

"*¿De donde viene el caballo?*" demanded Smith. "And where is the *yanqui* who rode it?"

The sullen brown jaw was tightly set, the eyes were flaring with anger. "*¿Quién sabe?*"

"You know and you're going to tell me about it. If you don't, I'll . . . I'll . . ." He felt in the pockets of his soggy shirt and found a box of matches. He struck one and looked at the goonie's feet. Then he knelt and began to remove a muddy leather puttee.

"No!" screamed the native. "No! I have heard what you do. I know you would torture me."

"That's better," said Smith and put the matches back in his pocket. "Where is this *yanqui*?"

"We wounded him. He is now on his way to our camp."

"What for?"

"He knows much, he is a great man. We would break him with certain means and obtain much knowledge. I went to bring other men."

"Which trail?" said Smith.

"One kilometer back, the trail to the left. But," added the goonie with a sick smile, "they have gone far, you can do nothing."

Smith stood up and looked back along the path. The native was right. He could do nothing about it now. In fact, it would be better if he did nothing. His orders were to the point. He had to avoid any such trouble. The orders were more important than a single man. The best he could do would be to tell them at camp and let the patrol take care of it.

But it was ten miles to Company K and in the meanwhile...

"One kilometer," said Smith. "I can see their tracks, anyway. I can make sure...."

To find out more about *Fifty-Fifty O'Brien* and how you can obtain your copy, go to www.goldenagestories.com.

Glossary

Glossary

STORIES FROM THE GOLDEN AGE *reflect the words and expressions used in the 1930s and 1940s, adding unique flavor and authenticity to the tales. While a character's speech may often reflect regional origins, it also can convey attitudes common in the day. So that readers can better grasp such cultural and historical terms, uncommon words or expressions of the era, the following glossary has been provided.*

---

auf Wiedersehen: (German) goodbye; until we meet again.

bandolier: a broad belt worn over the shoulder by soldiers and having a number of small loops or pockets for holding cartridges.

barker: someone who stands in front of a show at a carnival and gives a loud colorful sales talk to potential customers.

belaying pin: a large wooden or metal pin that fits into a hole in a rail on a ship or boat, and to which a rope can be fastened.

blackbird: to kidnap South Sea Islanders (Australian descendants from the more than eighty islands in the western Pacific) for use or sale as laborers.

black ivory: slaves.

bone: bone in the teeth; said of a ship speeding along sending up spray or foam under the bow. The phrase comes from the image of a dog, merrily running with a bone in its teeth.

• GLOSSARY •

boot: saddle boot; a close-fitting covering or case for a gun or other weapon that straps to a saddle.

bower of swords: the arch, or simulated shelter, formed by swords held by military personnel for the bride and groom to walk under as they exit the church.

cable length: a maritime unit of length measuring 720 feet (220 meters) in the US and 608 feet (185 meters) in England.

campaigner: campaign hat; a felt hat with a broad stiff brim and four dents in the crown, formerly worn by personnel in the US Army and Marine Corps.

Celebes Sea: a section of the western Pacific Ocean between the Indonesian island of Sulawesi (formerly known as Celebes), Borneo and the southern Philippines.

copra: the dried kernel or meat of the coconut from which coconut oil is obtained.

davits: any of various cranelike devices, used singly or in pairs, for supporting, raising and lowering boats, anchors and cargo over a hatchway or side of a ship.

¿De donde viene el caballo?: (Spanish) Where is the horse from?

Derringer: a pocket-sized, short-barreled, large-caliber pistol. Named for the US gunsmith Henry Deringer (1786–1868), who designed it.

Enfield rifle: any of several rifles formerly used by British and American troops, especially the .30- or .303-caliber, bolt-action, breech-loading model.

fantail: a rounded overhanging part of a ship's stern (the rear part of the ship).

flivver: a small, cheap and usually old car.

• GLOSSARY •

Flores Sea: a sea situated between the eastern end of the Java Sea and the western end of the Banda Sea in Indonesia.

fo'c's'le: forecastle; the upper deck of a sailing ship, forward of the foremast.

German East Africa: former German territory comprising present-day Burundi, Rwanda and mainland Tanzania.

gig: a boat reserved for the use of the captain of a ship.

give way: begin to row.

G-men: government men; agents of the Federal Bureau of Investigation.

grease: bribe or protection money; money given for corrupt purposes.

grifter: crooked game operator; a person who operates a sideshow at a circus, fair, etc., especially a gambling attraction.

guilders: Dutch coins. Guilder means *golden* in Dutch. The guilder originated as a gold coin (hence the name) but has been a common name for a coin of silver or other metal for some centuries.

gunwale: the upper edge of the side of a boat. Originally a gunwale was a platform where guns were mounted, and was designed to accommodate the additional stresses imposed by the artillery being used.

hawser: a thick rope or cable for mooring or towing a ship.

HE: high explosive.

Herr: (German) Mister, used as a title before a surname or profession.

Iron Cross of the First Class: a military decoration of the Kingdom of Prussia, and later of Germany, first awarded in 1813. The Iron Cross was awarded for bravery in battle,

· GLOSSARY ·

as well as for other military contributions in a battlefield environment. The Iron Cross First Class was a pin-on medal with no ribbon and was worn centered on a uniform breast pocket. It was a progressive award, with second class having to be earned before the first class and so on for the various degrees.

Kanakas: inhabitants of the South Sea Islands.

keel: a lengthwise structure along the base of a ship, and in some vessels extended downwards as a ridge to increase stability.

lam: to escape or run away, especially from the law.

le Maroc: (French) Morocco.

light out: to leave quickly; depart hurriedly.

longboat: the longest boat carried by a sailing ship.

lookout: a problem or concern.

midway: an avenue or area at a carnival where the concessions for exhibitions of curiosities, games of chance, scenes from foreign life, merry-go-rounds, and other rides and amusements are located.

monkey fists: ball-like knots used as ornaments or as throwing weights at the ends of lines.

Oberleutnant Kommandant: (German) chief lieutenant commandant.

pipe-clayed: made clean and smart; pipe clay is a fine white clay used in whitening leather. It was at one time largely used by soldiers for making their gloves, accouterments and clothes look clean and smart.

points: a point is 11.25 degrees on a compass, thus two points would be 22.50 degrees.

• GLOSSARY •

Prussian: a native or inhabitant of Prussia. Prussia, a former northern European nation, based much of its rule on armed might, stressing rigid military discipline and maintaining one of the most strictly drilled armies in the world.

Punch: the chief male character of the Punch and Judy puppet show, a famous English comedy dating back to the seventeenth century, by way of France from Italy. It is performed using hand puppets in a tent-style puppet theater with a cloth backdrop and board in front. The puppeteer introduces the puppets from beneath the board so that they are essentially popping up to the stage area of the theater.

puttee: a covering for the lower part of the leg from the ankle to the knee, consisting of a long narrow piece of cloth wound tightly and spirally round the leg, and serving both as a support and protection. It was once adopted as part of the uniform of foot and mounted soldiers in several armies.

¿Que pasó?: (Spanish) What happened?

¿Quién sabe?: (Spanish) Who knows?

quirt: a riding whip with a short handle and a braided leather lash.

Scheherazade: the female narrator of *The Arabian Nights*, who during one thousand and one adventurous nights saved her life by entertaining her husband, the king, with stories.

schooner: a fast sailing ship with at least two masts and with sails set lengthwise.

scupper: an opening in the side of a ship at deck level that allows water to run off.

Springfield: any of several types of rifle, named after Springfield, Massachusetts, the site of a federal armory that made the rifles.

• GLOSSARY •

Sulu Archipelago: island group in the Philippines lying between the Celebes and Sulu Seas. It includes over 900 volcanic islands and coral islets extending almost to Borneo.

superstructure: cabins and rooms above the deck of a ship.

tatterdemalion: raggedly dressed and unkempt.

Tawan: now Tawau; British-controlled town on the coast of Borneo facing the Celebes Sea. In the early nineteenth century, the British and Dutch governments signed a treaty to exchange trading ports that also divided Borneo into British- and Dutch-controlled areas.

.38 Colt: a .38-caliber revolver manufactured by the Colt Firearms Company, founded in 1847 by Samuel Colt (1814–1862) who revolutionized the firearms industry with the invention of the revolver.

top kick: a first sergeant, the senior enlisted grade authorized in a company.

two bits: a quarter; during the colonial days, people used coins from all over the world. When the US adopted an official currency, the Spanish milled (machine-struck) dollar was chosen and it later became the model for American silver dollars. Milled dollars were easily cut apart into equal "bits" of eight pieces. Two bits would equal a quarter of a dollar.

USMC: United States Marine Corps.

Very pistol: a special pistol that shoots Very lights, a variety of colored signal flares.

worse for wear: in poor condition; shabby.

yanqui: (Spanish) Yankee; term used to refer to Americans in general.

L. Ron Hubbard
in the Golden Age
of Pulp Fiction

*In writing an adventure story
a writer has to know that he is adventuring
for a lot of people who cannot.
The writer has to take them here and there
about the globe and show them
excitement and love and realism.
As long as that writer is living the part of an
adventurer when he is hammering
the keys, he is succeeding with his story.*

*Adventuring is a state of mind.
If you adventure through life, you have a
good chance to be a success on paper.*

*Adventure doesn't mean globe-trotting,
exactly, and it doesn't mean great deeds.
Adventuring is like art.
You have to live it to make it real.*

—L. RON HUBBARD

L. Ron Hubbard and American Pulp Fiction

BORN March 13, 1911, L. Ron Hubbard lived a life at least as expansive as the stories with which he enthralled a hundred million readers through a fifty-year career.

Originally hailing from Tilden, Nebraska, he spent his formative years in a classically rugged Montana, replete with the cowpunchers, lawmen and desperadoes who would later people his Wild West adventures. And lest anyone imagine those adventures were drawn from vicarious experience, he was not only breaking broncs at a tender age, he was also among the few whites ever admitted into Blackfoot society as a bona fide blood brother. While if only to round out an otherwise rough and tumble youth, his mother was that rarity of her time—a thoroughly educated woman—who introduced her son to the classics of Occidental literature even before his seventh birthday.

But as any dedicated L. Ron Hubbard reader will attest, his world extended far beyond Montana. In point of fact, and as the son of a United States naval officer, by the age of eighteen he had traveled over a quarter of a million miles. Included therein were three Pacific crossings to a then still mysterious Asia, where he ran with the likes of Her British Majesty's agent-in-place

• L. RON HUBBARD •

for North China, and the last in the line of Royal Magicians from the court of Kublai Khan. For the record, L. Ron Hubbard was also among the first Westerners to gain admittance to forbidden Tibetan monasteries below Manchuria, and his photographs of China's Great Wall long graced American geography texts.

L. Ron Hubbard, left, at Congressional Airport, Washington, DC, 1931, with members of George Washington University flying club.

Upon his return to the United States and a hasty completion of his interrupted high school education, the young Ron Hubbard entered George Washington University. There, as fans of his aerial adventures may have heard, he earned his wings as a pioneering barnstormer at the dawn of American aviation. He also earned a place in free-flight record books for the longest sustained flight above Chicago. Moreover, as a roving reporter for *Sportsman Pilot* (featuring his first professionally penned articles), he further helped inspire a generation of pilots who would take America to world airpower.

Immediately beyond his sophomore year, Ron embarked on the first of his famed ethnological expeditions, initially to then untrammeled Caribbean shores (descriptions of which would later fill a whole series of West Indies mystery-thrillers). That the Puerto Rican interior would also figure into the future of Ron Hubbard stories was likewise no accident. For in addition to cultural studies of the island, a 1932–33

LRH expedition is rightly remembered as conducting the first complete mineralogical survey of a Puerto Rico under United States jurisdiction.

There was many another adventure along this vein: As a lifetime member of the famed Explorers Club, L. Ron Hubbard charted North Pacific waters with the first shipboard radio direction finder, and so pioneered a long-range navigation system universally employed until the late twentieth century. While not to put too fine an edge on it, he also held a rare Master Mariner's license to pilot any vessel, of any tonnage in any ocean.

Yet lest we stray too far afield, there is an LRH note at this juncture in his saga, and it reads in part:

"I started out writing for the pulps, writing the best I knew, writing for every mag on the stands, slanting as well as I could."

To which one might add: His earliest submissions date from the summer of 1934, and included tales drawn from true-to-life Asian adventures, with characters roughly modeled on British/American intelligence operatives he had known in Shanghai. His early Westerns were similarly peppered with details drawn from personal experience. Although therein lay a first hard lesson from the often cruel world of the pulps. His first Westerns were soundly rejected as lacking the authenticity of a Max Brand yarn

Capt. L. Ron Hubbard in Ketchikan, Alaska, 1940, on his Alaskan Radio Experimental Expedition, the first of three voyages conducted under the Explorers Club flag.

(a particularly frustrating comment given L. Ron Hubbard's Westerns came straight from his Montana homeland, while Max Brand was a mediocre New York poet named Frederick Schiller Faust, who turned out implausible six-shooter tales from the terrace of an Italian villa).

Nevertheless, and needless to say, L. Ron Hubbard persevered and soon earned a reputation as among the most publishable names in pulp fiction, with a ninety percent placement rate of first-draft manuscripts. He was also among the most prolific, averaging between seventy and a hundred thousand words a month. Hence the rumors that L. Ron Hubbard had redesigned a typewriter for faster keyboard action and pounded out manuscripts on a continuous roll of butcher paper to save the precious seconds it took to insert a single sheet of paper into manual typewriters of the day.

That all L. Ron Hubbard stories did not run beneath said byline is yet another aspect of pulp fiction lore. That is, as publishers periodically rejected manuscripts from top-drawer authors if only to avoid paying top dollar, L. Ron Hubbard and company just as frequently replied with submissions under various pseudonyms. In Ron's case, the list

> **A Man of Many Names**
> *Between 1934 and 1950, L. Ron Hubbard authored more than fifteen million words of fiction in more than two hundred classic publications. To supply his fans and editors with stories across an array of genres and pulp titles, he adopted fifteen pseudonyms in addition to his already renowned L. Ron Hubbard byline.*
>
> Winchester Remington Colt
> Lt. Jonathan Daly
> Capt. Charles Gordon
> Capt. L. Ron Hubbard
> Bernard Hubbel
> Michael Keith
> Rene Lafayette
> Legionnaire 148
> Legionnaire 14830
> Ken Martin
> Scott Morgan
> Lt. Scott Morgan
> Kurt von Rachen
> Barry Randolph
> Capt. Humbert Reynolds

included: Rene Lafayette, Captain Charles Gordon, Lt. Scott Morgan and the notorious Kurt von Rachen—supposedly on the lam for a murder rap, while hammering out two-fisted prose in Argentina. The point: While L. Ron Hubbard as Ken Martin spun stories of Southeast Asian intrigue, LRH as Barry Randolph authored tales of romance on the Western range—which, stretching between a dozen genres is how he came to stand among the two hundred elite authors providing close to a million tales through the glory days of American Pulp Fiction.

L. Ron Hubbard, circa 1930, at the outset of a literary career that would finally span half a century.

In evidence of exactly that, by 1936 L. Ron Hubbard was literally leading pulp fiction's elite as president of New York's American Fiction Guild. Members included a veritable pulp hall of fame: Lester "Doc Savage" Dent, Walter "The Shadow" Gibson, and the legendary Dashiell Hammett—to cite but a few.

Also in evidence of just where L. Ron Hubbard stood within his first two years on the American pulp circuit: By the spring of 1937, he was ensconced in Hollywood, adopting a Caribbean thriller for Columbia Pictures, remembered today as *The Secret of Treasure Island.* Comprising fifteen thirty-minute episodes, the L. Ron Hubbard screenplay led to the most profitable matinée serial in Hollywood history. In accord with Hollywood culture, he was thereafter continually called upon to rewrite/doctor scripts—most famously for long-time friend and fellow adventurer Clark Gable.

In the interim—and herein lies another distinctive chapter of the L. Ron Hubbard story—he continually worked to open Pulp Kingdom gates to up-and-coming authors. Or, for that matter, anyone who wished to write. It was a fairly unconventional stance, as markets were already thin and competition razor sharp. But the fact remains, it was an L. Ron Hubbard hallmark that he vehemently lobbied on behalf of young authors—regularly supplying instructional articles to trade journals, guest-lecturing to short story classes at George Washington University and Harvard, and even founding his own creative writing competition. It was established in 1940, dubbed the Golden Pen, and guaranteed winners both New York representation and publication in *Argosy*.

The 1937 Secret of Treasure Island, a fifteen-episode serial adapted for the screen by L. Ron Hubbard from his novel, Murder at Pirate Castle.

But it was John W. Campbell Jr.'s *Astounding Science Fiction* that finally proved the most memorable LRH vehicle. While every fan of L. Ron Hubbard's galactic epics undoubtedly knows the story, it nonetheless bears repeating: By late 1938, the pulp publishing magnate of Street & Smith was determined to revamp *Astounding Science Fiction* for broader readership. In particular, senior editorial director F. Orlin Tremaine called for stories with a stronger *human element*. When acting editor John W. Campbell balked, preferring his spaceship-driven tales,

Tremaine enlisted Hubbard. Hubbard, in turn, replied with the genre's first truly *character-driven* works, wherein heroes are pitted not against bug-eyed monsters but the mystery and majesty of deep space itself—and thus was launched the Golden Age of Science Fiction.

The names alone are enough to quicken the pulse of any science fiction aficionado, including LRH friend and protégé, Robert Heinlein, Isaac Asimov, A. E. van Vogt and Ray Bradbury. Moreover, when coupled with LRH stories of fantasy, we further come to what's rightly been described as the foundation of every modern tale of horror: L. Ron Hubbard's immortal *Fear*. It was rightly proclaimed by Stephen King as one of the very few works to genuinely warrant that overworked term "classic"—as in: *"This is a classic tale of creeping, surreal menace and horror. . . . This is one of the really, really good ones."*

To accommodate the greater body of L. Ron Hubbard fantasies, Street & Smith inaugurated *Unknown*—a classic pulp if there ever was one, and wherein readers were soon thrilling to the likes of *Typewriter in the Sky* and *Slaves of Sleep* of which Frederik Pohl would declare: *"There are bits and pieces from Ron's work that became part of the language in ways that very few other writers managed."*

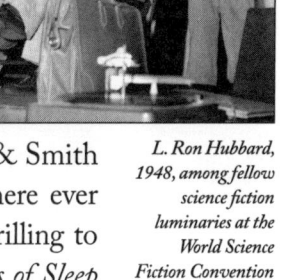

And, indeed, at J. W. Campbell Jr.'s insistence, Ron was regularly drawing on themes from the Arabian Nights and

L. Ron Hubbard, 1948, among fellow science fiction luminaries at the World Science Fiction Convention in Toronto.

so introducing readers to a world of genies, jinn, Aladdin and Sinbad—all of which, of course, continue to float through cultural mythology to this day.

At least as influential in terms of post-apocalypse stories was L. Ron Hubbard's 1940 *Final Blackout*. Generally acclaimed as the finest anti-war novel of the decade and among the ten best works of the genre ever authored—here, too, was a tale that would live on in ways few other writers imagined. Hence, the later Robert Heinlein verdict: "*Final Blackout is as perfect a piece of science fiction as has ever been written.*"

Like many another who both lived and wrote American pulp adventure, the war proved a tragic end to Ron's sojourn in the pulps. He served with distinction in four theaters and was highly decorated for commanding corvettes in the North Pacific. He was also grievously wounded in combat, lost many a close friend and colleague and thus resolved to say farewell to pulp fiction and devote himself to what it had supported these many years—namely, his serious research.

Portland, Oregon, 1943; L. Ron Hubbard captain of the US Navy subchaser PC 815.

But in no way was the LRH literary saga at an end, for as he wrote some thirty years later, in 1980:

"Recently there came a period when I had little to do. This was novel in a life so crammed with busy years, and I decided to amuse myself by writing a novel that was pure science fiction."

That work was *Battlefield Earth: A Saga of the Year 3000*. It was an immediate *New York Times* bestseller and, in fact, the first international science fiction blockbuster in decades. It was not, however, L. Ron Hubbard's magnum opus, as that distinction is generally reserved for his next and final work: The 1.2 million word *Mission Earth*.

> **Final Blackout** *is as perfect a piece of science fiction as has ever been written.*
>
> —Robert Heinlein

How he managed those 1.2 million words in just over twelve months is yet another piece of the L. Ron Hubbard legend. But the fact remains, he did indeed author a ten-volume *dekalogy* that lives in publishing history for the fact that each and every volume of the series was also a *New York Times* bestseller.

Moreover, as subsequent generations discovered L. Ron Hubbard through republished works and novelizations of his screenplays, the mere fact of his name on a cover signaled an international bestseller. . . . Until, to date, sales of his works exceed hundreds of millions, and he otherwise remains among the most enduring and widely read authors in literary history. Although as a final word on the tales of L. Ron Hubbard, perhaps it's enough to simply reiterate what editors told readers in the glory days of American Pulp Fiction:

He writes the way he does, brothers, because he's been there, seen it and done it!

THE STORIES FROM THE GOLDEN AGE

Your ticket to adventure starts here with the Stories from the Golden Age collection by master storyteller L. Ron Hubbard. These gripping tales are set in a kaleidoscope of exotic locales and brim with fascinating characters, including some of the most vile villains, dangerous dames and brazen heroes you'll ever get to meet.

The entire collection of over one hundred and fifty stories is being released in a series of eighty books and audiobooks. For an up-to-date listing of available titles, go to www.goldenagestories.com.

AIR ADVENTURE

Arctic Wings
The Battling Pilot
Boomerang Bomber
The Crate Killer
The Dive Bomber
Forbidden Gold
Hurtling Wings
The Lieutenant Takes the Sky

Man-Killers of the Air
On Blazing Wings
Red Death Over China
Sabotage in the Sky
Sky Birds Dare!
The Sky-Crasher
Trouble on His Wings
Wings Over Ethiopia

• STORIES FROM THE GOLDEN AGE •

FAR-FLUNG ADVENTURE

The Adventure of "X"
All Frontiers Are Jealous
The Barbarians
The Black Sultan
Black Towers to Danger
The Bold Dare All
Buckley Plays a Hunch
The Cossack
Destiny's Drum
Escape for Three
Fifty-Fifty O'Brien
The Headhunters
Hell's Legionnaire
He Walked to War
Hostage to Death
Hurricane
The Iron Duke
Machine Gun 21,000
Medals for Mahoney
Price of a Hat
Red Sand
The Sky Devil
The Small Boss of Nunaloha
The Squad That Never Came Back
Starch and Stripes
Tomb of the Ten Thousand Dead
Trick Soldier
While Bugles Blow!
Yukon Madness

SEA ADVENTURE

Cargo of Coffins
The Drowned City
False Cargo
Grounded
Loot of the Shanung
Mister Tidwell, Gunner
The Phantom Patrol
Sea Fangs
Submarine
Twenty Fathoms Down
Under the Black Ensign

• STORIES FROM THE GOLDEN AGE •

TALES FROM THE ORIENT

The Devil—With Wings *Pearl Pirate*
The Falcon Killer *The Red Dragon*
Five Mex for a Million *Spy Killer*
Golden Hell *Tah*
The Green God *The Trail of the Red Diamonds*
Hurricane's Roar *Wind-Gone-Mad*
Inky Odds *Yellow Loot*
Orders Is Orders

MYSTERY

The Blow Torch Murder *The Grease Spot*
Brass Keys to Murder *Killer Ape*
Calling Squad Cars! *Killer's Law*
The Carnival of Death *The Mad Dog Murder*
The Chee-Chalker *Mouthpiece*
Dead Men Kill *Murder Afloat*
The Death Flyer *The Slickers*
Flame City *They Killed Him Dead*

• STORIES FROM THE GOLDEN AGE •

FANTASY

Borrowed Glory
The Crossroads
Danger in the Dark
The Devil's Rescue
He Didn't Like Cats

If I Were You
The Last Drop
The Room
The Tramp

SCIENCE FICTION

The Automagic Horse
Battle of Wizards
Battling Bolto
The Beast
Beyond All Weapons
A Can of Vacuum
The Conroy Diary
The Dangerous Dimension
Final Enemy
The Great Secret
Greed
The Invaders

A Matter of Matter
The Obsolete Weapon
One Was Stubborn
The Planet Makers
The Professor Was a Thief
The Slaver
Space Can
Strain
Tough Old Man
240,000 Miles Straight Up
When Shadows Fall

• STORIES FROM THE GOLDEN AGE •

WESTERN

The Baron of Coyote River	*Man for Breakfast*
Blood on His Spurs	*The No-Gun Gunhawk*
Boss of the Lazy B	*The No-Gun Man*
Branded Outlaw	*The Ranch That No One Would Buy*
Cattle King for a Day	*Reign of the Gila Monster*
Come and Get It	*Ride 'Em, Cowboy*
Death Waits at Sundown	*Ruin at Rio Piedras*
Devil's Manhunt	*Shadows from Boot Hill*
The Ghost Town Gun-Ghost	*Silent Pards*
Gun Boss of Tumbleweed	*Six-Gun Caballero*
Gunman!	*Stacked Bullets*
Gunman's Tally	*Stranger in Town*
The Gunner from Gehenna	*Tinhorn's Daughter*
Hoss Tamer	*The Toughest Ranger*
Johnny, the Town Tamer	*Under the Diehard Brand*
King of the Gunmen	*Vengeance Is Mine!*
The Magic Quirt	*When Gilhooly Was in Flower*

Your Next Ticket to Adventure

Gun for the Action Behind Enemy Lines!

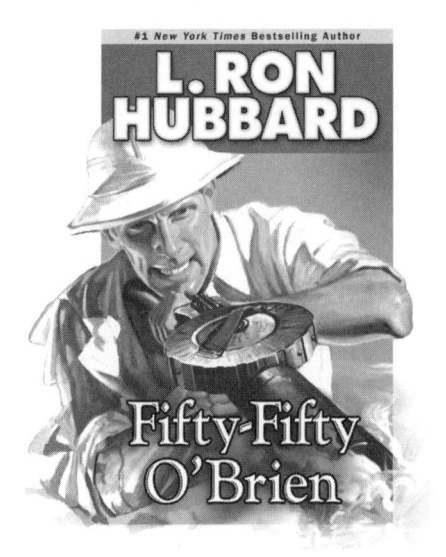

Winchester Smith is a crack shot. Problem is, his talent is going to waste, knocking down ducks in a shooting gallery. Win wants some real action, and like Gary Cooper as *Sergeant York*, he's going to war, joining the US Marines to fight in Central America. But serving as a messenger, he has little chance to put his rifle to use. When he does, he ends up facing a disciplinary hearing for disobeying orders. In order to redeem himself, Win will have to deliver a message that the Marines will never forget.

Step right up and take a shot as the audio version of *Fifty-Fifty O'Brien* leads you from the carnival midway to the middle of the jungle as a young Marine takes aim at heroism.

Get
Fifty-Fifty O'Brien

Paperback: $9.95 or Audiobook: $12.95

Free Shipping & Handling for Book Club Members
Call toll-free: 1-877-8GALAXY (1-877-842-5299)
or go online to **www.goldenagestories.com**

Galaxy Press, 7051 Hollywood Blvd., Suite 200, Hollywood, CA 90028

JOIN THE PULP REVIVAL
America in the 1930s and 40s

Pulp fiction was in its heyday and 30 million readers were regularly riveted by the larger-than-life tales of master storyteller L. Ron Hubbard. For this was pulp fiction's golden age, when the writing was raw and every page packed a walloping punch.

That magic can now be yours. An evocative world of nefarious villains, exotic intrigues, courageous heroes and heroines—a world that today's cinema has barely tapped for tales of adventure and swashbucklers.

Enroll today in the Stories from the Golden Age Club and begin receiving your monthly feature edition selected from more than 150 stories in the collection.

You may choose to enjoy them as either a paperback or audiobook for the special membership price of $9.95 each month along with FREE shipping and handling.

CALL TOLL-FREE: **1-877-8GALAXY**
(1-877-842-5299) OR GO ONLINE TO
www.goldenagestories.com
AND BECOME PART OF THE PULP REVIVAL!

Prices are set in US dollars only. For non-US residents, please call 1-323-466-7815 for pricing information. Free shipping available for US residents only.

Galaxy Press, 7051 Hollywood Blvd., Suite 200, Hollywood, CA 90028